IRON & LEAF

7 Turn Around Truths

Bob Miller, Ph.D., D.Min.

Iron & Leaf: 7 Turn Around Truths

2022 © Robert D. Miller

All rights reserved. No portion of this book may be reproduced, stored in a retrieval system, or transmitted in any form or by any means—electronic, mechanical, photocopy, recording, scanning, or other—except for brief quotations in reviews or articles, without the prior written permission of the author.

Limit of Liability/Disclaimer of Warranty: While the author may have used their best efforts in preparing this book, they make no representations or warranties with respect to accuracy or completeness of the historical accounts fictionalized in contents of this book. No warranty may be created offered or extended by any sales organization, distributor or event planner. The advice and strategies contained herein may not be suitable in all situations. Any reader should consult with a professional management consultant before applying the included principles in a business setting. Neither the publisher or author shall be liable for any loss of profits or any other commercial damages, including but not limited to special, consequential, or other damages.

Readers should be aware that Internet Websites provided quotes, historical accounts and source material through various information sources. Although these have been cited or referenced, they are credited as the source of original information that has been used in the fictional account.

It is the intent and purpose that the mention and use of tobacco products in this fictional work shall follow any and all legal age-limitations, federally, statewide and locally.

It is also noted that the Surgeon General of the United States has stated:

WARNING: Cigar smoking can cause cancers of the mouth and throat, even if you do not inhale.
WARNING: Cigar smoking can cause lung cancer and heart disease.
WARNING: Cigars are not a safe alternative to cigarettes.
WARNING: Tobacco smoke increases the risk of lung cancer and heart disease, even in nonsmokers.
SURGEON GENERAL WARNING: Tobacco Use Increases the Risk of Infertility, Stillbirth and Low Birth Weight.

First Printing, 10/2022

ISBN: 979-8-8468-8340-6

Cover Design by Jayden Wren

IronAndLeaf.com

Printed in the United States of America

IRON & LEAF

7 Turn Around Truths

Bob Miller, Ph.D., D.Min.

Famous Cigar Quotes

"I never smoke to excess—that is, I smoke in moderation, only one cigar at a time."
Mark Twain

"Some people meditate; I smoke cigars."
Ron Perlman

"I smoke ten to fifteen cigars a day. At my age, I have to hold on to something."
George Burns

"My boy! Smoking is one of the greatest and cheapest enjoyments in life, and if you decide in advance not to smoke, I can only feel sorry for you."
Sigmund Freud

"Given the choice between a woman and a cigar, I will always choose the cigar."
Groucho Marx

"There's something about smoking a cigar that feels like a celebration. It's like a fine wine. There's a quality, a workmanship, a passion that goes into the smoking of a fine cigar."
Demi Moore

"If you cannot send money, send tobacco."
George Washington

"Gentlemen, you may smoke."
King Edward VII of England

"Cheap cigars come in handy; they stifle the odor of cheap politicians."
Ulysses S. Grant

"I intend to smoke a good cigar to the glory of God."
Charles Spurgeon

"By the cigars they smoke, and the composers they love, ye shall know the texture of men's souls."
John Galsworthy

"There's a ritual about smoking a cigar that slows my clock down."
Matthew McConaughey

"Cigar smoking by its very nature is much more reflective than interactive."
Michael Douglas

"My favorite cigar is a free cigar."
Nelson Monteiro

"I am sure there are many things better than a good cigar, but right now, I can't think of what they might be."
Richard Carleton

"I think cigars are just a tremendous addition to the enjoyment of life."
Rush Limbaugh

To the cigar shop and lounge proprietors across the country, urban or rural, small and large, on Main Street or off side streets, you are heroes.

To my Brothers of the Leaf, at the end of the day, there is nothing that will divide us. Your love for a product that is born of seed and soil, aged and cured, crafted by hand, blended with passion and generously shared with others is without measure. Regardless of the shape, dimensions, country of origin or color of wrapper . . . each cigar is appreciated and admired. What a thought.

To Tierce, Bryan, John, Rick and all the team at Authentic Manhood, your mission to help men find their purpose through 33 has influenced me and helped impact others.

To those with whom I have sat and enjoyed a cigar, you have made me a better man, husband, father, grandfather, businessman and believer.

Table of Contents

Foreword *11*

Author's Comments *15*

Pete and The Sanctuary *17*

The Storm *23*

The Humidor Box *29*

Opportunity In Opposition – The Prime Minister *39*

Love What You Do – Gracie's Guy *47*

Look After Your People – The Coach *53*

Persistency Of Purpose – The General *61*

Get Going – The Storyteller *71*

Be Open Handed – The Pastor *79*

Fight Your Fear – The Champ *91*

Cleaning Up *99*

A Last Visitor *105*

Turn Around Truths *115*

The Back Story *117*

Acknowledgments *121*

Foreword

In 1992, I was working as an air traffic controller at Miami International Airport. I had a dream to start my own business, a family owned and operated cigar company. Out of my garage, my dad, Nick Sr. and I started Nick's Cigar Company. That same year, my wife, Janine and I welcome our first child, Nicholas III. That humble cigar company is now Perdomo Cigars, and my son is the next generation of family to lead our family business.

In our first year, Nick's Cigar Company sold 10,000 cigars. I was amazed. Soon after, the cigar boom of the 1990's exploded. In those humble beginnings, there were days when UPS would deliver bales of tobacco at my home and leaving them in the driveway because we were still growing and didn't have the production facility needed to sustain this fast-growing business.

In 1995, we moved our cigar production to Nicaragua. It was a big move . . . and it was the best move. Today, Perdomo Cigars' Nicaraguan facilities sit on 14 acres, with production and warehouse complex of over 750,000 square feet and over 1,200 acres of tobacco growing land. We are blessed to have almost 5,000 employees, while supporting approximately 20,000 Nicaraguans, and a production capacity of 80,000 cigars a day.

Janine and I have always instilled the importance of faith in God and family in our children. We have taught them to respect others and care for other, modeling the golden rule. If you live like that, life will always work itself out.

My father was a great businessman who was also a great cigar maker in Cuba. My uncle was also successful in business, including tobacco. And, my grandfather's brother was the minister of tobacco in Cuba for over 44 years. Our family has a heritage in cigars that I wanted it to continue.

In building a business, there are days of great encouragement as well as days of grueling discouragement. The motivation and passion of creating something with your own hands, either a growing business or rolling a great cigar requires a determination to never give up, to encourage others and to make a difference.

As a veteran, I learned the importance of resisting passivity and leading with courage. In the early days of Perdomo Cigars, I had to accept responsibility in order to keep things growing and moving forward. Every morning, we focused on what was needed for the day and what was needed for the future. We had to keep our eyes on tomorrow as we were working today while continue to build and honor our yesterdays.

Throughout life, I have learned to appreciate some of the great historical people who made an impact and contribution to society, but who also loved cigars. I think of Winston Churchill, Samuel Clemons, Ulysses S. Grant, Coach Red Auerbach and even the great Prince of Preachers, Charles Hadden Spurgeon. Spurgeon once said, "I intend to smoke a good cigar to the glory of God before I go to bed tonight." I wish it had been a Perdomo Cigar.

In his book, *"Iron & Leaf"*, Bob Miller draws from his own experience as a local brick & mortar cigar shop owner and identifies seven truths that have the power to turn situations around, in life and in business. He illustrates each truth through the stories and examples of various cigar lovers from the pages of history . . . men that we all know . . . and some great cigars. These great cigar aficionados inspire, encourage and challenge the reader to be real and authentic with simple and powerful truths.

I had the pleasure of meeting Dr. Bob Miller many years ago, having an event at two of his shops in central Virginia. The power of these truths was illustrated in his commitment to his craft and customers.

His passion for his family, friends, customers and his faith reminded me how similar Bob and I are, quite honestly. We both have been blessed with long marriages, wonderful children and we are grandparents!

When Bob asked me the honor of writing the foreword, I simply couldn't resist because I know that this book would be very interesting and more importantly, a great read. Bob truly radiates positivity and compassion to everyone he meets.

Appreciate this book knowing that it truly communicates the three most important things in my life hope, confidence and optimism. Please enjoy.

Nick Perdomo
President, **Perdomo Cigars**

Author's Comments

"Iron & Leaf", is an unconventional and uncompromising story of redeeming time and turning a life, business, and passion around.

Pete is at a crossroads. He has helped other struggling businesses, but he can't seem to help himself. He's just not able to find the right strategies to turn his own passionate business.

Although this story is a work of fiction, there are some real events that have shaped the characters and needed truths.

I have always had a fascination with the unique bond of cigars. Throughout history, those who appreciate cigars share a commonality and connection. The characters in this book are somewhat familiar to many. They are noted cigar aficionados of their day and time. And, some were known to have a passion for cigars, illustrated in their folklore and contributions to history. Each character contributes an insight of truth that can have an impact. The Prime Minister, Gracie's Guy, The Coach, The General, The Storyteller, The Pastor and The Champ are all contributing authors to the nuggets of inspiring and life changing truth.

Many of the historical accounts found in "Iron & Leaf" have been researched and supported by sources found through the World Wide Web and Wikipedia. Many of the quotes are credited as being from the source.

This book may have undertones of faith. For that, I unashamedly confess that it is intentional. In my years of owning a cigar shop and attending many, I agree with Blaise Pascal, "There is a God-shaped vacuum in the heart of every man which cannot be filled by any created thing, but only by God the Creator, made known through Jesus Christ." It was always my hope and intent to show Jesus to those with whom I enjoyed cigars.

It is my hope and prayer that this book will be an encouragement to those who struggle with the burdens of life. It will communicate hope, confidence, optimism, and expectation.

Pete and The Sanctuary

Pete was an eccentric entrepreneur.

For over five decades, he successfully acquired businesses that were broken or busted. When it came to economic development, he was a "jack-of-all-trades". Self-taught in finance, marketing, sales, management, and customer service, he had ample expertise to be effective, but lacked lasting experience to be sustaining. Yet, with determination and diligence, he brought small businesses back to life.

Some could only be saved for a short time. Others survived and thrived. These financial resurrections had been turned over and entrusted to the hands of young business moguls who worked hard, hustled and were hungry.

Pete was eccentric because he was unconventional. He was an entrepreneur because he was uncompromising. Being unconventional, he always thought outside the box. Being uncompromising, Pete usually challenged traditional business models and approaches. Just because it had always been done a certain way, did not mean it was the best way. Pete had a different approach . . . a different box. Unconventional and uncompromising.

Breathing new life into a dying business brought new hope. Every new sale, invoice, and customer became a reviving pulse indicating that healing and strength were on the horizon.

Pete loved the envisioning of business. He also loved cigars.

Cigars tend to be unconventional and uncompromising, as well. Unlike other tobacco products, these handmade "works of art" require years to reach market availability and customer appreciation.

Originating with a simple seed that contains legacy and life is just the beginning. Many of the current crops of cigar tobacco in other countries, have their genesis in Cuban cigar tobacco seeds dating back generations. These seeds are planted in countries like Nicaragua, the Dominican Republic, where the tobacco grown from the original Cuban seeds, yield other seeds that share a rich lineage.

Those planting, caring for and growing the seed often unknown and underappreciated. The heart of the grower and the heritage of the seed . . . that's where the unconventional takes root.

Those first seeds, being surprisingly small, were most likely smuggled out of Cuba by cigarmakers seeking relief during the pre-Castro takeover in the 1960s. Little seeds, easily hidden or disguised, were guarded, and protected with extreme care.

From the flowers at the crown of a tobacco plant, priceless and delicate seeds are harvested. These seeds are potted and as they germinate and grow, after one or two weeks, they eventually become seedlings only a few inches in height.

Tobacco grows rapidly.

In just two months, most seedlings grow strong enough that they can be soil-planted. After another ninety days, plants mature and are approximately twenty-million times heavier than the seed. During the growing time, specific amounts of nitrogen, potassium, and magnesium are added when the soil is lacking.

Then there is the watering. It has been said that watering tobacco needs the "Goldilocks" strategy . . . not too much . . . not too little . . . it has to be just right. In the Pinar del Rio region of Cuba, the sandy soil and humid environment averages two inches of rainfall per month. This is the standard. This is the guideline. It is uncompromising.

You can get the soil right. You can be precise with watering. But it doesn't stop there. Every day, plants need to be examined, protected from hungry insects, and pruned. While tobacco is growing, it must be clipped and tarnished, having smaller unwanted leaves removed. Low hanging leaves are pruned. Flowers are picked. Because of their height and weight, support from wood or wire ensures they remain straight and tall, reaching for the heavens and soaking in the sun.

Fully matured tobacco leaves are harvested and spend at least another sixty days barn-curing and fermenting. Fermentation can last for weeks, months, or even years. Large piles or "pilones" of leaves are stacked and restacked repeatedly as heat and moisture purge the leaves. Impurities, harshness, and by-products are eliminated.

After fermentation has done its magic, leaves are layered and compressed into drying bundles that weigh several hundreds of pounds. The tobacco is stored in a warehouse where the aging process begins, slowly maturing over weeks, months, and years.

Massive warehouses holding years of harvested tobacco ensure that cigars made today are just as flavorful as those of the past.

In a world of quick turnarounds and bargaining quality, Pete appreciated the unconventional approaches and the uncompromising commitment of the cigar industry.

It's been said that if you can find something that you love and earn a living doing it, your work will never be a job . . . it will be a joy.

Pete had his eye on a building off Main Street in the downtown area of the city. After peering through the curved display windows framed by locally quarried greenstone, his interest was peaked wondering if this could be a cigar shop.

The building had been constructed in the early 1900's. It served several purposes from a five-and-dime to a clothing emporium to a jewelry store. It was long and narrow. The walls were early century plaster that had chipped off and revealed red brick from the shared wall of the next-door building.

The front single door was hinged to swing in and out. It was a single plate glass door, weighty and majestic; also framed with greenstone on both side panels. The entrance was even more impressive with the glass and brass door handle, massive and masculine.

The floor was dull and covered with warn carpet and padding that was at least twenty years old. But, underneath revealed small, Italian marble tiles that had been imported by the original builder. Beautiful shades of ivory, green and rose formed patterns of regality and masterful craftsmanship.

This was the place for Pete's dream to become reality. This was the place to forge his own business . . . not someone else's that needed saving . . . but his own empire. This was the place his passion for cigars would intersect with his purpose in life.

This was the place where Pete could not only build an investment, but also invest in the lives of patrons and customers. This could be a place where "iron sharpens iron". This was a "band of brothers" shop.

This was the place. It was unconventional and it would be uncompromising. This was it.

Pete didn't waste any time negotiating a lease on the building. Papers were signed. Keys were received. The work began.

Additional areas of brick were exposed to give it an upscale warehouse feel. Upon entering the shop through the stately glass door, the right side plastered walls were painted a forest green color that created an atmosphere of soothing calm.

The left side of the building housed a newly constructed walk-in humidor. The interior wall was forty feet long and ten feet wide, the five ten-foot-high and eight-foot-wide sections of Spanish Cedar each held six shelves, slightly tilted to display cigars. A flat top-shelf was used for storage and backstock. Pete always wanted to have "one to show and one to go"; one on the shelf to sell as individual sticks and one up top to sell an entire box. In total, almost 400 boxes of cigars could be presented for any customer's selection and enjoyment. The exterior wall of the humidor was a handsome combination of Mahogany wainscoting and glass. The humidor was entered through a single, glass paneled door. Each shelve was illuminated with accenting lights to showcase the cigar. A humidification unit ensured the proper humidity and temperature.

It was regal. It was grand. It was handsome. It was perfect.

Carpet was pulled up. Floors were cleaned, buffed and shined.

Accent rugs were selected. Pictures of industrial period cigar factories and rolling Torcedors hung on the walls.

Three sections of comfortable and deep leather chairs were positioned in the lounge area, on the left side, adjacent to the brick exposed wall. Each section had eight chairs: one at the head, one at the foot and three on each side. In the middle of the chairs was a simple, but well-appointed marble coffee table. Between every two chairs, was a small pedestal ash bowl.

Lighting was subtle yet inviting. Filtration fans hung from the twenty-foot ceiling, each with a mid-century globed lamp.

Display cases and racks were toward the rear of the shop. These held accessories, pipes, pipe tobacco and humidors for purchase. The register area was next to the humidor and allowed full view of all those who entered.

On the back wall, near the entrance to the restroom, hung a large American flag. This flag had seen its years of wear, but still symbolized the weighty meaning of freedom and liberty. On the wall behind the register area there were photos of famous cigar lovers throughout history. When Pete's concept for the shop began to take shape, he wondered about the role cigars had played throughout history. And, who really enjoyed cigars. As he researched, he found so many names: Churchill, Kennedy, Grant, Groucho, George, Milton, Auerbach, The Babe and even Charles Hadden Spurgeon . . . men from every walk of life and from every period of time. The commonality was that whatever their station in life, they shared a common passion. The cigar. The images of these men were now displayed on the wall. Five rows of five . . . twenty-five men who love cigars. These men were truly brothers of the leaf.

Pete established accounts, met with cigar sales reps, and began placing orders to fill the humidor. His selections were thoughtful and strategic, combining traditional and legacy brands with accents of boutique. Within weeks, the humidor was filled and ready for customers.

The last addition to the shop was the classic cigar Indian. Placed just outside the entrance to the humidor, the traditional icon of early century cigar shops found its place.

In 1667, King Charles II passed a law which forbade the use of overhead signs because of the danger presented to passing pedestrians. As early as the 17th century, European tobacconists used figures of American Indians to advertise their shops.

The wood for cigar Indians was typically white pine, purchased as logs at lumber yards. The wood sculptor first blocked out a very rough outline by axe, guided by paper patterns. A hole was then bored into each end of the log, about five inches in depth, and a bolt placed into each. The log was then suspended from these bolts on supports so it could freely turn. The sculptor would use chisels, followed by finer carving tools, to create the finished figure. Arms and hands were created separately, then screwed into the body. The last steps were to paint it and set it up upon a stand.

Pete's cigar Indian held a bundle of cigars in his left hand, with his right hand shielding his eyes from the sun as if looking toward the horizon. A beaver pelt rested over his right shoulder. This cigar Indian wore a chief feather headdress. He had a knife in a sheath on his hip. The sculpture rested on a faux, carved rock base.

With everything in place, Pete needed a name. A moniker to identify this haven for lovers of the leaf. An identifier for all who shared his passion for cigars.

This was his dream. This was his place of rest. This was his sabbath place. This was his sanctuary. And that was it . . . The Sanctuary.

It was a place of refuge from life's weariness. It was a place of safety from the attacks and pressures of every single day. It was a place of reverence honoring the holiness of brotherhood and sisterhood. It was a place of honoring the work of all that goes into the creating of a cigar . . . the artistry, the craftsmanship, the skill.

Sacred. Safe. Secluded. Sanctuary.

The Storm

The cigar business is challenging. For some, owning a brick-and-mortar store is a hobby. If they can make a few bucks here and there and have access to some of the best cigars available. What could be better?

But it's inevitable. Eventually, a hobby moves from enjoyment to employment . . . from the "relaxing" to a "routine" . . . from wonder to work. Hours of operation. Customers. Employees. Sales forms. Sales Tax. Tobacco Tax. Income Tax. Payroll. Inventory. Marketing. Social Media. It can be exhausting and endless.

Pete had helped other businesses, small and large, simple and complex, through some challenging times and transitions. He was skilled with the ability to comprehend multiple complex issues and summarize them with simple, workable and cost-savings solutions.

His favorite quote was attributed to Andrew Jackson, seventh President of the United States. Jackson said, "I was born for the storm, and the calm does not suit me."

Before taking the oath of office, Jackson had fought thirteen duels. In the War of 1812, he marched 2,000 Tennessee Volunteers from Nashville to New Orleans. During the march, 150 soldiers became gravely ill, of which 56 could not even stand. Dr. Samuel Hogg asked General Jackson what he wanted to do, and Jackson replied, "You are not to leave a man on the ground."

This is the origin of the mandate, "Leave no man behind."

Pete had helped other business owners who felt lost or left behind. His insights and encouragement gave others the courage to run "into" a storm, not run "from" it. And, if possible, to withstand the adversity and to wait it out with courage and confidence, having a competent plan in place.

Pete was now in his own storm. He was coming up on five years with The Sanctuary. He had built a slowly growing business, but not a great, and at times, not even a good business. There were times that it was floundering.

Finances were tight. In reality, finances for a small business are always tight. Pete had used most of his savings and he was familiar with spending on credit . . . cards, home equity, family loans. Pete would have a good month and then unplanned expenses would come up.

Inventory was also a task to manage. Items that sold or turned quick were easy to replenish. But there were always those cigar brands that guests would request and they would just sit on the shelf. Pete found that he often had to offer specials or cut deals to get enough cash flowing. Those cut into his profits.

There was always something to repair or replace. And those ate into the profits. Guests who experienced a damaged cigar, cigars that were dropped in the humidor, or even a regular guest who didn't like a certain cigar . . . all of these hit the bottom line.

He had good employees and loyal customers. Employees, however often didn't accept the responsibility or have the attitude of an owner, simply because they were not the owner. And some customers could never be satisfied. The cigars weren't humidified correctly, the lighters didn't work, they couldn't find a cutter or prices went up on their favorite cigar. Pete often said that when doing something to appease a customer's concern; the first time they will appreciate it, the second time they will expect it and the third time they will insist on it.

Pete's neighbors were also a frustration . . . the businesses located right next door to The Sanctuary. Although the shop had superior ventilation and air exchangers, the neighbors didn't care for cigar smoke. They felt it was inappropriate and damaging to the community. They had expressed their concerns to the local government, but of no avail. The city understood that he had expeditiously followed the required guidelines and requirements. Pete was frustrated in his ability to make a difference in his own community.

The grind of every day was beginning to take its toll. Pete could help others with short-term strategies and solutions, but he rarely considered the "long-game" of running a business. Now he was in the long-term phase . . . the "hang of the grip" phase and his hands were slipping.

For the first time in his life, Pete had a hard time sleeping, eating and relaxing. The cigars started being too many and the shots of spirits were too frequent.

Now the storm was building in intensity and strength. Pete wasn't sure if he could keep the business going or if he even wanted to. It was five years on a roller-coaster and the end of the ride was quickly approaching. There were some moments when he didn't want to make any other decisions. Just sit back, enjoy a cigar, smoke all those in the humidor and let it happen. He wanted to just let it go, but he couldn't. This was his dream. This was his destiny.

He needed something to help him do his own turnaround. Something to help guide his thoughts in moving forward and to guard his heart from any discouragement.

These thoughts pelted Pete's mind every day. Like the sound of rain hitting a metal roof, he was reminded of the storm. He needed to do something.

Over the past few years, Pete found his spot to sit each and every day. It was at the section of chairs nearest to the sales center and next to the humidor. He chose the chair at the head. From this seat, Pete could see the entire humidor and the front door. He could spot any customer, either entering or shopping.

Pete knew his customers by name. He was good at that. When they entered, he would say, "Hey, Joe. Welcome to The Sanctuary. I'm here to make your day great." The only challenge was on a sunny day. When someone entered through the heavy, plate glass door the illuminating brightness created a shadowed silhouette. The shape of some patrons was recognizable. But others could only be identified once the door closed.

Shadowed profile or recognizable face, Pete would greet them the same way, "Hey, my friend. Welcome to The Sanctuary. I'm here to make your day great."

Every day was a learning day. Meeting new people, engaging in discussions, and asking provoking questions always brought new insights and considerations. It was amazing what you learn in a cigar shop.

At the end of each day, when the final customer had left, Pete would examine the humidor and make adjustments to the inventory and shelf space. After closing, this became his time to think about the day, reflect on the conversations with customers and process the good and the not so good.

In showcasing the varieties of cigars, each manufacturer had their allocated space in the humidor. The best sellers had eye-level and top shelf space. Others filled in the lower shelves. When a box was left with one or two cigars, Pete would claim those for his tomorrow smoke. Pete's one or two cigars were called his "stragglers". He would place them in his pocket and then retrieve a box from the flat top shelf to fill the empty space.

A small, and at times wavering three step ladder was used to reach up top. Pete was not a short man, but his just over six-foot height still needed to stretch to reach cigar boxes at the very top shelf. There were times when his acrobatic like stretches, balancing two or three boxes in one hand with leg extended to get the last few inches of reach caused a balancing act full of comedy and concern.

Pete finished most of the inventory facings. The shelves looked well stocked and organized. There was just one more spot that needed just the right box. And that box was at the very top of the backstock shelf, stacked on several others. Pete placed the unpredictable step ladder, climbed each step carefully until he was at the summit, and like a skilled puzzle piece mover, stacked and restacked boxes to finally reach the one that he needed.

With one final stretch, as Pete's fingertips touched the cigar box, his toes shifted from the step ladder. In trying to minimize his fall, he reached out to grab the closest shelf. Boxes were flying and he was falling. It seemed like someone had turned on a slow-motion camera. As the floor was getting closer, Pete felt a thud near his right ear. As he landed on his back, his head felt like it bounced off the ivory, rose and green Italian marble tile.

He laid there on the floor in a ten by forty-foot walk-in humidor, made of Spanish cedar, wainscotting of Mahogany and glass. Boxes that, just a few minutes before were precisely positioned on the shelfs had now toppled next to him. His arms and legs seemed to be okay. Nothing was broken. His back was stiffening. His pride was yelling at him for not being careful. And his head was throbbing. He felt the right side of his head, the hairline near his ear and it was moist with just the slightest bleeding. Nothing on the back of his head but a large, bulging bump.

As he pulled his knees in, sat and gathered what thoughts he could, he could feel the heavy humidity of this cigar room contributing to his increasing perspiration.

He could hear the humidification unit running with the sound of a gentle breeze. From his low position, the lights in the humidor were bright and the lights in the lounge area of the shop were dimming.

Pete needed to get up.

He tried to stand but had to sit back down. Frustrated. Embarrassed. Anxious. Humiliated. Pete knew the longer he sat, the harder it would be to get up.

Pete clinched his teeth, pursed his lips, and rolled over to get on all fours. He secured one foot on the floor and the other knee as a support. He placed his hands on a shelf and ledge, looked up to the ceiling and pulled to stand up.

And, then the lights went out.

The Humidor Box

Even with his eyes closed, Pete was aware that he was no longer on the floor. He was sitting in a chair. He felt luxurious and smooth leather. The chair was soft, comfortable, and cushiony. He felt as though he was enveloped in relaxing comfort.

Music was playing. It was a soft Jazz. The kind of music that unintentionally causes you to lightly tap your finger as it dances in your head and makes you smile.

The air was familiar. It was cool, refreshing and had a scent of cigar smoke. Not offensive but calming. Not overwhelming but reassuring.

Pete was a bit apprehensive to open his eyes. Had he "checked out"? Had he "passed on"? Had his metaphorical cigar finally gone out? Had he tapped the final ash?

With his eyes still closed, Pete slowly moved his right hand from the arm of the chair to the back of his head. He thought that if the bump was still there and it hurt, then he had not yet moved the last piece of life's chess game. The bump was still there, and it hurt. It really hurt.

Pete opened his eyes and saw that he was still in The Sanctuary. Somehow, he had moved from the humidor to the lounge area. He was sitting in his seat, at the head of the first section of eight chairs, facing the glass door and next to the walk-in humidor.

He could see through the glass into the humidor. The shelves were straightened, and all the cigar boxes were in place. The top shelf had been organized. And the unreliable, unfaithful, and unforgiving three-step ladder was leaning against the wall.

Pete couldn't figure out was had happened. Had he been able to pick everything up and then just sat for a bit to relax. Had one of his employees come in and cleaned up the overnight mishap? Did it really happen at all?

As confusion was getting ready to take a prominent position in Pete's thinking, the heavy and weighty plate glass front door to The Sanctuary opened. He couldn't tell who it was because of the bright, early morning sun shining from the outside. All he saw was the shadow of man, dressed in a suit, and what look like a box being carrying under his right hand.

As was his habit, Pete said with a bit of uncertainty, "Hey, my friend. Welcome to The Sanctuary. I'm here to make your day great."

Pete stood, oddly with great ease and lack of stiffness, stretched out this hand and introduced himself. The man, speaking with a kind and gently southern accent introduced himself as Michael.

Michael was a bit older that Pete. He was a dark-skinned man with a comforting and welcoming smile. A trimmed mustache and goatee, with hints of gray accented a strong chin. Michael's eyes were comforting, perceptive and engaging.

His hands revealed that he was a laboring man. They were calloused, but gentle. His handshake had a reassuring grip. His shoulders indicated that he could carry a heavy physical load, as well as a caring and burdensome weight. It was evident that Michael worked hard and was fit, yet, he evidenced a possible fondness for food evidenced by a slight overhang of his belly over his belt.

He was dressed in light tan linen trousers; a light blue oxford stripped button-downed collar shirt with a royal blue bowtie, and a royal blue linen blazer, studded with brass buttons, as well as a tan and light blue pocket square.

Michael wore a complimenting straw Panama style hat, light tan with an accenting band that matched his pocket square. Upon removing his hat, his smooth, cleanly shaven, hairless head was revealed.

And Michael's shoes were something Pete hadn't seen for a while. Saddle shoes. Blue and white with interlacing blue and white shoelaces. The straw Panama hat and the shoes were handsome and bespoken.

It was evident that this man enjoyed cigars. The aroma wafting from his attire was familiar and inviting.

Michael carried a felt bag. It was the size of a small duffle bag, but rectangular in shape. It was a deep and royal purple color. Pete was curious of the bag.

Pete set aside his curiosity and asked if he could help Michael with anything. Michael said, "It seems you have a wonderful selection of cigars. If I select one, will you join me?" Pete rarely had someone buy a cigar for him, so he was grateful.

Pete responded, "That would be very appreciated, sir. What can I get you?" Michael asked if Pete had a cigar made by the Padron family. "Anything from the Thousand Series. Preferably a Maduro."

Pete smiled and said, "How does a Padron 3000 sound?" "Great choice", Michael replied with a beaming smile.

They sat in the first section of seating near the back, next to the humidor. Pete sat at the head chair with Michael to his left. Michael placed the felt bag in the chair next to him. The men slid their cigars from the cellophane wrappers. Michael retrieved his cutter and lighter from his coat jacket. Pete used the table cutter and lighter.

As they lit their cigars, Pete asked Michael why he chose the Padron Thousand series. Michael answered, "Well, my friend. These are excellent cigars, with exceptional quality and a fair price. Every time I have one, they are consistent in flavor, burn well and last long enough to have a meaningful chat. And the cigar name reminds me of one of the many reasons I love cigars. There are thousands of lessons one can learn from other cigar lovers. A first cigar with a special friend or son. Celebrations. Reflections. Victories. Defeats. Every cigar has a story. Every story has a hidden lesson. Every lesson has a simple truth that can turn a life around."

Pete had never thought about all the lessons he had learned from others in his own shop. He learned a lot of new information, but turnaround truths were a different way to look at it. This was something he needed to consider.

Michael took a puff on his cigar, slowly exhaled the cloud of billowing smoke, followed the smoke as it dissipated into the ceiling fan, and reflectingly turned to Pete, "This is an amazing place with an incredible ambiance. Tell me why you wanted to open a cigar lounge and why is called The Sanctuary?"

Pete, also tracing the path of cigar smoke, smiled, took another puff on this cigar and said, "I love working with people and I appreciate cigars. I thought if I could combine the two, it would be incredible."

Michael smiled and said, "Do what you love and love what you do." Pete nodded his head and continued, "But there's another reason. For most of my life, I was a 'loner'. I was intuitive enough to figure things out on my own. But there were times I could have used the insight from an "wise older owl" type of person. I'm not being disrespectful in any way. There is great wisdom and insight from someone who is a bit further down the road from you."

Now Michael was nodding in agreement and his smile was encouraging Pete to continue. "A wise King from ancient Jewish history once wrote, 'Iron sharpens iron, so a man sharpens another.'", he said. "I wanted to have a place where men could come, enjoy a cigar, be encouraged and learn from others. To some, its mentoring. To others, its coaching. To me, it's a sacred trust and opportunity. It's iron on iron. Brothers helping brothers."

Pete became more impassioned, "This place is not only a place to enjoy a cigar and meet the guys; it's a place to learn how to be a better person, a better friend, a better member of your family, a better member of your community. It's a place where you can understand what it takes to be an authentic and real man. This place is a refuge. A shelter. A sanctuary. That's what we call it . . . The Sanctuary."

Pete suddenly forgot about the challenges of his business and about the earlier fall. Michael's question helped him remember why he wanted to open his cigar shop.

Michael looked at Pete with a probing stare. Not uncomfortable, but reassuring, inviting, and engaging. He asked, "So, Pete, how is it going? Are your patrons being encouraged? Do you see 'iron sharpening iron'?"

Pete took a puff of his cigar, looked up to the ceiling and exhaled. His eyes met Michael's eyes and he said, "It's not going well. No. They are not being encouraged. And, no, I don't see anyone being sharpened. I've gotten so caught up with the challenges and problems of my business that I've lost sight of why I started it."

Michael didn't say anything. He just waited. Pete took another puff on this cigar, a little slower and a little deeper, exhaled and said, "Michael, I've spent most of my adult life helping businesspeople and entrepreneurs get back to their purpose and passion. I've helped them see how they have gotten off track and guided them to get back on course. They usually know how. They just need to be reminded of the lessons they have learned."

"What did you call them earlier? Turnaround truths?" Michael nodded in affirmation.

"That's what I need." Pete said, softly and introspectively, "Turnaround truths". Pete ashed his cigar, looked at Michael and said, "Enough about me. I'm curious about you. And you must tell me . . . what's in the felt bag?"

Michael raised his eyebrows, smiled, rested his cigar on the nearest ashtray and reach in the chair next to him, reverently holding the purple felt bag.

"Before I can show you what's in the bag, I would like to tell you a story." Michael's gaze became warmly intense and focused. He gently picked up his Padron 3000, took a long, steady draw on his cigar, slowly exhaled the smoke, and turned his attention to Pete.

"My ancestors are from the Congo River region in Africa. They were brought across the Atlantic as slaves to the States. The ship that transported them was unique because it was owned by the family on whose plantation they worked and lived." Michael continued, "The Shepherd family not only raised crops, including tobacco, they also had a mill that processed trees for furniture and construction. The ships from the Congo region primarily carried harvested timber, exclusively Mahogany, as well as a select number of slaves, skilled in lumbering and wood."

This was an unknown historical fact to Pete. In fascination, he leaned in to learn more.

As Michael went on, his voice carried a deliberate and steady tone, "No doubt, the Shepherds were slave owners. Yet, they treated those under their estate with care and compassion. Housing was very modest. Meals were not extravagant, but there was enough. They worked hard and long hours. But there was always dignity and stewardship."

As he took another puff on his cigar, Michael said, "My great-grandfather was given the name, "Solomon" by Mr. Shepherd. He always thought that my great-grandfather had a 'special' kind of insight. The two would talk often."

Michael looked just over Pete's shoulder, as if staring into the distant. "I remember hearing stories of Mr. Shepherd reading from the Holy Book every morning, specifically The Proverbs. My great-grandad would tell me as a young boy, 'There are thirty-one sacred proverbs. One for each day. A proverb a day will keep the devil away.'", Micheal chuckled.

"Many slave owners were cruel and harsh. Mr. Shepherd demonstrated wisdom, discernment and understanding. I believe it was because of the Proverbs." Michael paused, looked at Pete and leaned forward as to intensify the next words to be spoken. "Mr. Shepherd spent time talking to a slave, Solomon. My great-grandfather asked Mr. Shepherd, 'Sir, why do you take time to talk with me and tell me about the holy things from the Divine?'"

Michael's voice began to quiver, "Mr. Shepherd would tell him these words, 'Iron sharpens iron, so one man sharpens another.'" Pete's chair almost grabbed him as he sunk back. He eyes looked up as into the heavenlies and then looked at Michael. Both of their eyes were moistened with utter wonder.

Michael, with a tender, yet powerful tone said, "You know, Pete. With that statement, Mr. Shepherd recognized my great-grandfather as a man. Not just an ordinary man, but a man who had value and contribution. That was Mr. Shepherd."

He went on, "My family was given their freedom, as well as a small portion of the Shepherd's land. They continued to serve the Shepherd's for the next fifty years . . . no longer as slaves, but as neighbors and co-laborers."

"My grandfather and father both became craftsman of wood, mostly Mahogany from Africa. They made furniture, hope chests, and fine desktop boxes." Micheal said in a more relaxed voice.

He paused, looked at Pete and unfolded the purple felt bag. Pete moved to the edge of his cushion chair in anticipation. Micheal pulled out a wooden box, much the size of a small humidor.

Micheal held it with both hands, as if it were a royal crown on a stately pillow. The box was not that large, maybe the size of a small file box. It looked to be twelve inches long by eight inches deep and five inches tall. It was a dark and deep wood.

The corners had ornate silverish, metalwork on each corner of the top. There was an emblem on top of the same material.

Micheal looked at the box and said, "This wood is from the regions of the Congo in Africa. It is as old as a legacy. It has withstood times of poverty and prosperity. It is known for its straight grain and dark color." He continued with a reverent tone in his voice, "The ornate symbols on each corner are made of silver from the first coins earned by my grandfather. Each is shaped as an angelic messenger looking up and symbolizing hope." His expression became more deliberate, "The emblem on top is from the same silver and is inscribed with the words, 'Iron On Iron, Brother To Brother'."

As he opened the humidor, Pete was expecting to see some type of wood, possibly Spanish Cedar. Instead, it was lined with copper, with seven cigars neatly placed inside. Michael explained, "In the early 1900's copper was readily available and was a non-reactive metal that could be used to inhibit bugs from damaging cigars. Over the years, copper has come to symbolize human nature, its justification and perfection. The patina of copper shows a beauty with change."

Michael sat back in his chair with the cigar humidor on his lap, "My grandfather made this humidor by hand, using wood that came over from Africa harvested from the same ship that transported my great-grandfather. The copper is from a teapot used by my great-grandmother. The silversmith work is by my grandfather. And the emblem was crafted by my father. I was given this humidor almost a half-century ago."

As he gently ran his hands over the humidor, Michael spoke very reflectively, "This humidor reminds me of strength, purity and change. Each part has been turned from a raw material into an element of purpose. Truth, with strength and purity always brings about positive change."

Pete was silent and still. His mind was processing all that Michael said. His heart was pounding. For The Sanctuary and its future, he knew he needed a renewed strength to move forward. He needed a purity of purpose. And he needed some kind of change.

Michael placed his hands on each side of the humidor, looked at Pete and extended his arms. "Pete, its time." Pete was unsure what Michael meant. Was it time for him to leave? Pete slightly tilted his head as to communicate his question. Michael continued, "Its time for me to leave", he paused, "And Its time for me to leave you this humidor."

Pete was silent, caught between shock and wonder.

Pete quickly responded, "No, Micheal. I could never accept such an incredible heirloom. It's your family's treasure. They've been through so much and this humidor carries a part of each of them." But Micheal insisted, "My friend, I have no one left in my family. You are a newly found brother. And you have brought a smile to my face, today. I have been reminded of importance of the lessons taught by my great-grandfather, grandfather, and father. I want you to have this humidor. I believe it may help you discover the strength, purity and change that is needed for the next part of your life."

Michael stood and handed Pete the humidor. As Pete accepted it, he was speechless. Michael straightened his royal blue bowtie, and gave a tug to the hem of his royal blue linen blazer, and adjusted the tan and light blue pocket square.

He placed the straw light tan Panama style hat to cover his smooth, cleanly shaven, hairless head. He took his hand and ran his fingers over the brim of the hat and slightly tilted one side.

He folded the purple felt bag and placed it under his left arm, while extending his right hand to Pete for a shake. Pete gripped Michael's hand and their eyes locked. The handshake transitioned into a hug.

If was a brief, but meaningful embrace. Pete felt as if a brother had visited and was ready to leave. As they began separate, he asked Michael about the seven cigars in the humidor. Michael, with his hands on Pete's shoulders, said, "Give them to the next seven customers who come in. Tell them that an old gentleman wanted to bless some friends, today."

Pete nodded as Michael clicked the heels of his blue and white saddle shoes with interlacing blue and white shoelaces, and began whistling as he walkout through the heavy, plate glass door of The Sanctuary.

Michael's unique style soon faded into a shadowed silhouette.

Pete sat down in his chair, at the head of eight seats, just in front of the sales area and next to the walk-in humidor. In his lap, he held the humidor entrusted to him by Michael.

As he ran his hands over the surface of the humidor, his thoughts drifting to a time when a large ship journeyed from the coast of Africa to the colonies of the United States, carrying a cargo of slaves and wood.

He opened the humidor with seven cigars inside, seeing the orange and green tinted copper and considered the power of change.

His fingers touched the ornate corners and he wondered if Michael's message of encouragement was exactly what he needed. And he looked at the emblem. Michael had taught Pete some valuable lessons that left a positive impression and impact. Micheal was iron sharpening iron. Michael was a brother to a brother.

Pete drew the humidor closer to his chest . . . closer to his heart. He gently closed his eyes and went a bit deeper in thought. In his hands and close to his heart was a gift.

A humidor made of Mahogany, dark in color with straight grains from the regions of the Congo in Africa. As old as a legacy, withstanding times of poverty and prosperity. Lined with copper, with a rich patina of truth, purity and change. Ornate symbols on each corner made of precious silver, each shaped as an angelic messenger looking up symbolizing hope. And an emblem on top inscribed with the words, "Iron On Iron, Brother To Brother".

Pete's deep thought was interrupted by the familiar sound of The Sanctuary's large vintage front glass door swinging opened.

Opportunity In Opposition – The Prime Minister

No matter where he was in the cigar lounge, Pete could hear the door opening. It was weighty. It was majestic. It was announcing, in its own way, that someone was there who may need to have a great day.

The bright light of the early morning still darkened the detail of who was entering The Sanctuary. Although shadowed images can be deceiving, the silhouette clearly outlined a shorter, rounder man. Pete could tell that he was well dressed, wearing a hat similar to German styled Homburg and carrying an umbrella.

He walked with confidence and authority.

As the gentleman came closer, Pete was fascinated with the quality and detail of his clothing. This stately man was wearing a three-piece chalked-pinstriped suit made of a very dark charcoal flannel fabric. The suit was indicative of some of London's Seville Row tailors. His neatly pressed white shirt was complimented with black bow-tie, highlighted with white polka-dots.

Pete couldn't help but look up and down, admiring the man's style from head to toe, including the black leather laced boots, which were highly polished. And, he was wearing a gold watch chain, draped between his waistcoat pockets.

As Pete began to stand, he said, "Hey, my friend. I'm Pete. Welcome to The Sanctuary. I'm here to make your day great."

The gentleman whimsically smiled, and in an orator's, voice said, "Thank you, kind sir. The name is Churchill, Winston Churchill."

For one of the first times in his life, Pete was speechless. Had the bump on the head been more serious that he thought? Was this actually happening? Or, was this a dream? A hallucination? A vision?

He didn't have time to figure it out. Mr. Churchill . . . wait, Mr. Churchill? Mr. Churchill was standing in front of him.

Not being accustomed to moments of silence, Churchill asked, "Are you the proprietor of this fine establishment, sir?" Pete, still not knowing what to say, simply nodded. "Well then, sir, I believe it would be enjoyable, if not beneficial to have a morning cigar."

Although Pete was still unsure of what was taking place, he knew that he had a shop full of cigars and Mr. Churchill wanted to start his day with a cigar. That was a great recipe for a great day.

Pete motioned for Mr. Churchill to sit in the same seat where Michael sat, just seemingly a few moments ago. Mr. Churchill removed his Homburg, leaned his umbrella next to his chair and with an inquisitive look, turned toward Pete. "I trust it has been a grand start for the day, sir?" Pete said, "Yes, sir." And, without thinking, Pete said, "Your suit is very handsome. Not many men take the time or make the effort to wear this kind of suit, today." As soon as he said it, Pete felt a bit underdressed in his jeans, camp style shirt and casual shoes.

Without missing a beat and with a whimsical smile and a twinkle in his eye, Churchill replied, "Well sir, we are all worms, but I do believe that I am a glowworm."

Pete chuckled and said, "Well played, sir. Well played." Churchill nodded in agreement.

With a slight anxious tone, Churchill asked, "So, my friend, what shall we smoke?"

Immediately, Pete paused. He was getting ready to make a recommendation to one of the greatest statesmen of all time. Pete looked to the right at the forty-foot humidor, seeing his shelves full of inventory through the spotless glass dividers.

Pete shifted his gaze from the walk-in humidor to Mr. Churchill and then back to the Michael's humidor. He remembered Michael's instruction about the cigars in the humidor, "Give them to the next seven customers who come in. Tell them that an old gentleman wanted to bless some friends, today."

Pete looked at Mr. Churchill and said, "A brother of the leaf was here earlier today. He asked me to bless some friends with the gift of a cigar. May I give you one from his collection?"

Churchill slightly grinned, nodded his balding head and said, "Thank you, sir. I would be honored to accept such a kind and heartfelt gift."

Pete leaned forward in his chair and opened the humidor. Inside, Pete saw seven cigars. He recognized all of them. Some expensive and some not. Some new and some well-loved with years. Each one had a band and none were wrapped in cellophane. Each one was distinct and each one had a story.

Pete reached inside and saw an Ashton Prime Minister. And, he thought, "what a perfect cigar for Mr. Churchill".

As Pete handed him the cigar, he said, "Sir, this is a cigar from the Dominican Republic and it's called the Prime Minister. It's made by Ashton. It's binder and filler are Dominican, while the wrapper is a golden-blond Connecticut Shade grown leaf. Some say it is mild in its strength, but strong in its flavor. Most savor nuances of toasted almonds and coffee beans, with a hint of sweetness. I believe it's a vitola you prefer, almost 7 inches, with a ring gauge of 48. Many call this size a Churchill."

Mr. Churchill smiled and said, "See my friend, being a glowworm has it's privileges." He laughed in a very dignified manner, but you could tell he was enjoying himself. Mr. Churchill reached in his waistcoat pocket and pulled out a cigar punch. Once he cut a perfectly round hole, he reached in the other pocket and retrieved a box of wooden matches. After toasting the cigar, he took a long draw, tilted his head back and released the whitish smoke.

Pete reached in his pocket and pulled out a cigar. Pete always had several cigars in his pocket. They were usually one or two left from an open box. In Pete's thoughts, it was better to see a full box on the shelf, as opposed to an almost empty box. Those "stragglers" found their way into Pete's pocket.

Mr. Churchill enjoyed another puff and said, "Sir, I wish I had the palate that you possess. It is curious to me that I simple enjoy the taste of tobacco. I am a simple man with simple tastes."

Pete dropped his head and smiled. As he cut and lit his own cigar, he said, "Yes, sir. I have a hard time picking up those flavors, also. But I do enjoy a good, smooth cigar."

Mr. Churchill, smiled, nodded and took another puff.

Pete's mind quickly remembered some things that he had heard or read about this gentleman.

Born in 1874, Churchill's family was part of the British aristocracy. Attending private schools, he eventually gained admittance to the Royal Military Academy at Sandhurst. While serving as President of Board Trade, in the early 1900's, Churchill introduced a bill that prohibited miners from working more than an eight-hour day. He also helped establish the concept of a minimum wage and the right of workers to have meal breaks.

Churchill was appointed the First Lord of the Admiralty. During the war, he vowed that Britain would build two warships to every new battleship built by the Germans.

As a British leader during the Second World War, he was inspirational as a noted statesman, military office, historian, author, artist and even an amateur bricklayer.

Noted as an animal lover, Churchill bred butterflies, keeping them in a converted summerhouse until the weather was acceptable to release them. He had several pets, mainly cats, but also dogs, pigs, lambs, bantams, goats and fox cubs, He was often quoted as saying that "cats look down on us and dogs look up to us, but pigs treat us as equals."

He is the only British Prime Minister to receive the Nobel Prize in Literature.

As Pete and Churchill continued to enjoy their cigars, Mr. Churchill began to inquire about Pete, The Sanctuary and the handsome humidor sitting on the table in front of them.

"Well, Mr. Pete. How are you getting along in this wonderous enterprise? Is this not every man's dream?"

Pete smiled and thought that sometimes this dream can be a bit of a nightmare. He didn't want to bear his burdens with the Prime Minister. But, something about Mr. Churchill was inviting. He was engaging and encouraging. He was insightful and intuitive. He was deliberate and decisive.

Pete began talking about helping others with there businesses, but not being able to get his off the ground. He told Mr. Churchill that he thought The Sanctuary would have more customers by now. That it would be more profitable. That more men would find it a place to belong.

Mr. Churchill sat and listened. He nodded at times. Leaned forward to engage and he would lean back to reflect. All, while managing to smoke his cigar with a meaningful enjoyment.

Churchill looked at Pete and said, "My friend, continuous effort, not strength or intelligence, is the key to unlocking our potential. Too often, we seek immediate success or gratification. We often look for the least difficult means to accomplish the most difficult tasks and then we give up when it gets too difficult. Don't give up, my friend."

Pete was hanging on the Prime Minister's every word. Here was a man who stood in the face of Nazism, and provided words of inspiration and hope to a nation on the brink of devastation.

Churchill continued, "The pessimist sees difficulty in every opportunity. The optimist sees opportunity in every difficulty. I've learned in many of my battles, with enemies, as well as with those across the aisle in Parliament, that the opportunity for success lessens when we lose enthusiasm. My dear friend, success is going from failure to failure without losing enthusiasm."

Pete could feel hope bubbling up. He had allowed minor setbacks to have a major impact.

Churchill leaned forward, looked Pete squarely in the eyes and said, "Now, Peter, this is not the end. It is not even the beginning of the end. But it is, perhaps, the end of the beginning. This is a new path on life's journey for you."

Mr. Churchill and Pete continued to talk. Pete was inspired. And, yes, Churchill was inspirational. As their time went on, their cigars became less and less.

Mr. Churchill had nothing more that a nub left on his cigar. He took a final puff and looked at Pete. Pete knew their time was about to end. He still didn't know if this was a dream or a hallucination. But Pete knew the impact of his time with the Prime Minister was real.

Churchill looked at Pete and said, "In 1941, I was invited to a boarding school where I had been enrolled as a young boy. During my visit to Harrow School, I was asked to say a few words. This was a difficult and challenging time for the United Kingdom. Although many felt that we were in dark days, I felt we were in great days. I told these young men that these are the greatest days of our country has ever lived; and that we must all thank God that we had been allowed, each of us allowed to play a part in making these days memorable."

Pete was listening intently and recalled hearing highlights of his speech. Churchill continued, "These are the words that were born in my heart with which I challenged the next generation, 'Never give in, never give in, never, never, never . . . in nothing, great of small, large or petty . . . never give in except to convictions of honor and good sense."

Pete could hear the intensity build with every use of the word, "never".

Churchill leaned forward in his chair, looked Pete in the eyes and said, "My dear friend, success is not final. Failure is not final. It is the courage to continue that counts. Be assured that there is always opportunity in every opposition. Never give in. Never give up."

The only amount left on Mr. Churchill's cigar was the band that read "Ashton".

Pete was trying to remember all of Mr. Churchill's timely and powerful encouragement. How could he share this with others? He reached out and touched the Prime Minister's arm and said, "Sir, could you leave me a just a few words to remind me of our time together?"

Mr. Churchill reached in his suit pocket, retrieving a fountain pen. He took the Ashton cigar band, turned it over and wrote, "Never Give Up". He handed it to Pete and said, "My friend, may these three words give you hope and encouragement."

The Prime Minister stood, and offered his hand in brotherhood and friendship to Pete. Pete looked at him and said, "Iron sharpening iron". Mr. Churchill smiled and said, "That's what men do."

Mr. Churchill placed his Homburg on his head, grabbed his umbrella, placed his right hand on his hip and walked out through the plate glass door.

Pete waited until Mr. Churchill's image faded from the view of the door. He sat down in his comfortable leather chair with Michael's humidor on his lap and cigar band from the Ashton Prime Minister in his hand. He turned the band over, read the words again, "Never Give Up" and was encouraged.

He lifted the lid and placed the cigar band inside with six remaining cigars. He looked at the humidor, once again admiring the craftsmanship. He gently rubbed in hands over the lid, touching each of the corners.

A humidor made of Mahogany, dark in color with straight grains from the regions of the Congo in Africa. As old as a legacy, withstanding times of poverty and prosperity. Lined with copper, with a rich patina of truth, purity and change. Ornate symbols on each corner made of precious silver, each shaped as an angelic messenger looking up symbolizing hope. And an emblem on top inscribed with the words, "Iron On Iron, Brother To Brother".

Love What You Do – Gracie's Guy

As Pete sat in his chair, resting the humidor on his lap, he wondered, again, if this was a dream. It was obvious to him that Mr. Churchill passed away. So, was he dreaming? Had the bump on the head been more than just a bump? Was he awaiting entrance through the eternal gates and was this something that helped prepare his heart, mind and soul?

He was becoming very reflective, as well as restful. Whatever this was, it calmed Pete. It caused him to be less anxious about the challenges before him and more appreciative of where his life's journey had brought him. His time with the Prime Minister helped him rethink some things. His thoughts were turning around from helplessness to hope.

As Pete was deep in thought, a familiar sound brought him back to reality and the surroundings of The Sanctuary. The large and heavy plate glass door was opening and Pete stood and looked to see another shadowed outline of a small framed man.

While Mr. Churchill walked in with determination and purpose, this man's steps were light and happy. And, he was very small in stature and quite thin.

As he walked into the shop, he was humming an old-style vaudeville type tune. Pete couldn't name it, but it was familiar.

As he came closer, it was evident that his man had his own fashionable style. The gentleman wore a navy blazer, camel-colored trousers, and a blue pinpoint shirt with no tie. And, he was wearing light brown leather loafers.

Pete could tell that this man's grey, almost white hair was an indication of his age. He wore round framed glasses and his eyebrows slightly arced over the lenses, giving an appearance that his eyes were smiling. And, he was smiling. Not a big smile, but a light-hearted, mischievous grin.

Pete energetically said, "Hey, my friend. I'm Pete. Welcome to The Sanctuary. I'm here to make your day great."

In a confident and spry tone, the man replied, "Good morning. Gracie told me about a great cigar shop in this part of town. I hope this is the right part of town. The wrong part doesn't have a great cigar shop." And, he warmly smiled with the corner of his mouth rising. "My name is Nathan . . . Nathan Birnbaum. But people have a hard time remembering that name. So, I usually tell my name is George. George Burns."

Mr. Birnbaum, or Mr. Burns looked around, gently patted his blazer pockets, spread his arms out to his side, turned to see the walk-in humidor and said, "Well, it looks like you have a few cigars. Brother, can you spare a dime and get me one?'

Pete smiled and thought, "This is going to be some kind of day".

He looked at the gentleman and said, "Well, George, Gracie was right. I hope you find this to be a great cigar shop. We call it The Sanctuary. I believe I have the perfect cigar for you. Please have a seat here." Pete motioned to the same chair that just a short time ago was occupied by Britain's greatest Prime Minister.

As George sat in the comfortable leather chair, it almost seemed to swallow him. Pete sat, leaned forward and opened up the humidor. Inside were six cigars and Churchill's cigar band. One of the cigars was something Pete had not seen for years. He wasn't sure he had ever carried it in his shop. But he knew the cigar. Pete reached in and pulled out an El Producto Queens.

The Queens was the cigar Burns used in all of his stage performances. Although he could choose any cigar he wanted, including any Cuban brands, the El Producto Queens was the one cigar that would stay lit during his entire stage show. He was often teased by Milton Berle, Sid Caesar, Ernie Kovacs and other top entertainers, asking him to move up to Havanas. But Burns stated that the Queens would always be his cigar of choice.

A ten-a-day cigar smoker, Burns would receive a shipment at his Beverly Hills residence, of 300 Queens a month, each packaged in a glass tube. When introduced, the Queens were a handmade premium blend of Havana and Puerto Rican tobaccos.

As Pete reverently presented the Queens cigar, George's smile became more evident, his eyes widened and his hand graciously accepted it. "Hello, old friend. Yes, sir! Gracie was right again. You know, Pete, Gracie is always right. She used to tell me that, often."

Pete reached in his pocket and pulled out another cigar. Pete cut his cigar using a V-cut and George popped off the cap of the Queens. Pete offered to light both cigars. Each of them took a deep draw, sat back in their chairs in unison and gently blew out the smoke.

"So, George, tell me a little bit about you. What's it like being one of the greatest comedians of all time?", Pete asked, cutting through all of the levels of awkwardness. He thought, if I'm not sure what's going on, maybe he doesn't either.

George didn't bat an eye. "Exhausting", he said, "There's an old saying, 'Life begins at forty.' That's silly. Life begins every morning you wake up. And you always wake up. Well, most mornings, at least. It's that last one that will kill you." George smiled and looked at Pete from the corner of his eyes.

"I know you may not believe this, Pete. But, I'm one hundred years old. When I was a boy, the Dead Sea was only sick." George paused just the exact right moment to create the perfect comedic timing. "Pete, I must say that this is a very nice place. And, it's nice to be here. Actually, at my age it's nice to be anywhere . . . and, know that you're there."

Pete found it challenging to puff his cigar, laugh and not choke on the smoke.

George focused on Pete, shyly smiled and dropped the ash on his Queens. He took a deliberate draw on his cigar, blew out the smoke and said, "Pete, this is a beautiful cigar shop." Looking around and taking in every area of The Sanctuary, he said, "So, Pete, do you love it? Do you love having each and every day filled with cigars?" George waited for Pete to answer, enjoying his cigar and patiently anticipating a response.

"Yes, sir. I love it, Mr. Burns", George gently interrupted, "Please, call me George. The doorman calls me Mr. Burns. My chauffeur calls me Mr. Burns. The guy who gives me a massage calls me Mr. Burns. You? A man who owns a cigar shop and gave me a cigar, today? You call me George. In fact, you can even call me Georgie-boy. Well, no you can't. Gracie wouldn't like that. Just call me George."

Pete grinned and took a puff on his cigar, "It's probably one of my favorite things in the world. I love cigars. I love the people. I love the chance that guys have to come in, talk and get to know each other. I love the way they joke around with each other. I love the laughter. I love the honest conversations. Yes. I love it."

George heard Pete's words, but he also heard something else in his voice. He said, "That's great, Pete. You know, I have gotten really good at reading an audience, over the years. I sense there's something you're not saying. Come on. Tell it to Georgie. Out with it."

Pete smiled, "I love it. But what if I fail? What if I can't make this shop work? What if I . . . ". George leaned forward in his chair, held his El Producto Queens in his right hand and said, "Fall in love with what you do for a living. To be able to get out of bed and do what you love to do the rest of the day is beyond words. Son, I honestly think it is better to be a failure in something you love than be successful at something you hate."

Pete nodded his head in agreement. He wasn't sure his heart was in agreement, though. "What about all the other demands in life? Family? Marriage? How do you balance it all?" Pete's voice was impassioned. He loved his business and he loved his loved ones.

George leaned back into his chair, "Lots of people have asked me what Gracie and I did to make our marriage work. And, Pete, I miss her dearly. It's simple. We didn't do anything. Too many people work too hard at staying married. I think the trouble with a lot of people is that they think marriage is like a business and they make a job out of it. When you work too hard you get tired; and when you get tired you get grouchy; and when you get grouchy you start fighting; and when you start fighting, you're out of business."

"I say love what you do and love who you're with . . . as long as you're doing your job and you're loving your wife." George said, with a twinkly in his eye that clearly indicated the spark in his heart. "Never forget an anniversary or birthday. Show her love and appreciation. And, always be encouraging. With small words and in big ways."

Pete agreed and George continued, "You forget a lot of things over the years. First you forget names, then you forget faces. Next you forget to pull your zipper up and finally, you forget to pull it down." Pete laughed hard.

"You know, Pete. There is one thing you should forget. Forget what has happened in the past. Enjoy the encouragement of your friends and family. They will make you a better man. They will hone you and help you, like iron sharpens iron. And, look to the future because that's where you're going to spend the rest of your life."

George looked up toward the ceiling, took a puff of his cigar and smiled. And, with his left hand, he reached down to make sure his zipper was still up.

As both men were finishing up their cigars, George leaned back and began taking the band off his Queens and said, "Forget what has happened in the past. Plant seeds for the future. Enjoy the encouragement of your friends and family. And look to the future because that's where you're going to spend the rest of your life. Don't take the journey alone. Take others with you. Speak words of hope, not hurt. Always be kind. Encourage others."

Pete quietly said, "Can I ask you to do me a favor, George?" He nodded and said, "Of course, anything." Pete continued, "I want to remember your visit and your meaningful words. Could you take your cigar band, turn it over and write two or three words that I can use to remember today?"

George reached in the left chest pocket of his navy-blue blazer, took out a pen and wrote, "Encourage Others" on the back of the El Producto Queens cigar band and handed it to Pete with the wink from his eye.

Pete smiled, with the corners of his eyes being moist with tender appreciation. He opened up the lid of the humidor and place the cigar band inside.

With a curious inquiry, George said, "That's a beautiful humidor. And, it looks almost as old as me." Pete respectfully chuckled and nodded. "What's its story?"

Pete took a few minutes to tell George about Michael. He told him of the encouragement of the Shepherds, the impact on Michael's family, and the gift of an amazing humidor given to him.

And, for the first time in their visit, George was speechless. He only said one thing, "Gracie would have loved that story."

Both men stood, shook hands and then hugged. George looked at Pete and said, "You were given a world and everything in it. It's all up to you."

Pete smiled remembering that line between John Denver and George in the movie, "Oh God!"

George fastened the middle button of his blazer, saluted, put his left hand in his pocket turned and walked out into day. Pete's eyes followed him as he faded into the brightness of the sun.

As Pete began to clean up, his mind was processing the insight of two different men who shared practical wisdom and passion. Emptying the ashes and wiping down ashtrays, his eyes focused on the gifted humidor.

A humidor made of Mahogany, dark in color with straight grains from the regions of the Congo in Africa. As old as a legacy, withstanding times of poverty and prosperity. Lined with copper, with a rich patina of truth, purity and change. Ornate symbols on each corner made of precious silver, each shaped as an angelic messenger looking up symbolizing hope. And an emblem on top inscribed with the words, "Iron On Iron, Brother To Brother".

Pete walked around the sales counter to the sink and began to wash out the cleaning cloths. He heard the plate glass door open and he looked to see who was entering.

Look After Your People – The Coach

Still unable to see the detail of who was entering The Sanctuary, Pete could make out the silhouette. It was a dark outline of a person with a blinding brightness behind them. It's almost like they were walking out of pure light.

Pete could tell it was a man, probably middle aged. He looked just under six feet, a bit heavy and quite a receded hairline. And, he walked with purpose and intentionality; not too fast, but just the right pace to show that he had control of the floor.

As he moved closer to the sales area, Pete could see that he was wearing a wide-lapeled, green and white plaid sport coat, dark trousers, white shirt and a very wide green tie patterned with little shamrocks.

He stood in the middle of The Sanctuary, hands on his hips, surveying the seating area and walk-in humidor. He looked in Pete's direction and said, in a very Eastern New England accent, "This is a nice 'cigah' place. Yep. Very nice."

Pete smiled and said, "Hey, my friend. I'm Pete. Welcome to The Sanctuary. I'm here to make your day great."

The gentleman smiled with a welcoming and inviting grin, reached out his hand and said, "Well, thank you, sir. My name is Red. Red Auerbach."

As Pete shook his hand, he said to himself, "This is crazy. Churchill. Burns. And, now Red Auerbach. I think I may like this kind-of-crazy." And, then he remembered one of the things that George said, "Take each day as it comes."

Pete looked at Mr. Auerbach and said, "Coach, can I get you a cigar? I'm not sure, but I believe I have one you may like. You see, a recently made friend of mine gave me this beautiful gift." Pete motioned to the humidor resting on the coffee table in front of Pete's chair. "My friend left some cigars in the humidor and said, '"Give them to some of your customers who come in. Tell them that an old gentleman wanted to bless some friends, today.'"

Red smiled and said, "Well, Pete, I must be blessed with the luck of the Irish."

Pete motioned for the Coach to sit in the same chair as his two previous distinguished guests. Pete sat in his normal spot, reached for the humidor and opened it. Inside were five cigars and two cigar bands. The bands had the words, "Never give up" and "Encourage others", each in a distinctive and unique handwriting.

As Pete selected the cigar for Coach, he chose a Hoyo de Monterrey, Red Auerbach's signature cigar. Pete couldn't take his eyes off the cigar as he handed it to his guest. How? What? Pete didn't have the answers to the dozens of questions running through his mind. He was just going to take this day as it came.

Hoyo de Monterrey cigars began in 1865. These cigars are noted for being a full-flavored Honduran cigar blended with Nicaraguan, Honduran and Dominican filler. Complimented with a Connecticut binder and wrapped with a flawless and superb Ecuadorian Sumatra wrapper, this cigar is full of flavor and character.

Red looked at the cigar, smiled, ran the cigar under his nose and said, "Ah, yes. A victory cigar. The fans in the Garden would love this."

Pete reached in his pocket and pulled out another cigar. He offered to cut each cigar and Coach accepted. Pete ignited his cigar with a lighter in his pocket. Coach used the table lighter. Both men, toasted the ends of their cigars, continued to light and simultaneously, each took that first, long puff. And, each man released a satisfying sigh, exhaling a billow of smoke.

Pete remembered watching NBA games on Sunday afternoons, as a boy. The intense series involving the Boston Celtics were legendary. Bob Cousy. John Havlicek. Tommy Heinsohn. Bill Sharman. Sam Jones. Tom "Satch" Sanders. K.C. Jones. And, Bill Russell. All amazing All-Star players coached by Red Auerbach.

As coach of the Celtics for over 15 years, Auerbach won ten Eastern Division championships, as well as nine NBA titles, including eight straight. After retiring from coaching, he continued to serve as General Manager and President. He's been named NBA Coach of the Year, NBA's All-Time Team Coach and the Greatest Coach in the History of the NBA. He was also the author of seven books.

In all of his accomplishments, his most significant was creating "Celtic Pride". Players, coaches, front office and fans of the team weren't allowed to be "fair-weathered". They would bleed green and stand on principles of tradition, hard work, perseverance and team, "forever and always". This was the essence of "Celtic Pride."

Red Auerbach was also famous for lighting up a Hoyo de Monterrey as a victory cigar, before the game ending buzzer. He always lit the cigar when the Celtics were ahead and the game was out of reach. The Boston fans loved it and opposing teams loathed it. Opponents saw it as a sign of disrespect, but Red kept on lighting them up. His own players often had a sigh of regret because the lighting of Red's cigar motivated the opposing team to be more competitive. In spite of it, the Celtic fans and the television audiences embraced this tradition. It created a sense of pride and drama. When the Fleet Center banned smoking, they made an exception for Red Auerbach.

In addition to his knowledge and love of the game of basketball, Red also had a friendship and love for his players. He often referred to the Celtics as having a "family feeling." Most notably was his friendship with five-time NBA MVP, Bill Russell. Red was white. Bill was black. Red grew up in the Williamsburg area of Brooklyn, playing ball in the streets. Bill grew up in West Monroe, Louisiana, playing ball on every level. Although they were different, Red Auerbach believed in Bill Russell. And with the love of brothers, a relationship of coach and player developed into an impacting and influential force.

As Pete looked over at Red Auerbach, savoring his cigar, with his leg crossed and remembered that those days of basketball and its superstars were golden years.

Pete took a puff on his cigar and asked, "So Coach Auerbach, what brings you into our cigar shop?", not knowing how he would answer.

Coach looked at his cigar, took another puff and said, "Pete, I'm not real sure. I don't want to be alarming. But the last thing I remember was taking a walk and thinking about my blessed life. The good times and the bad times. And, the great people that have been a part of my life. I briefly closed my eyes, said a brief prayer of gratitude and appreciation. When I opened my eyes, I was standing outside of that large plate glass door to your shop. I could smell the wonderful aroma of cigars. I decided to walk in. And, now I'm here with you enjoying a great cigar."

Pete nodded and said, "Well, Coach. I'm sure glad you decided to stop in. It's been an interesting day with some incredible customers." Trying to keep the conversation going, Pete asked, "Are you still coaching?"

Red looked at Pete like he was crazy. Pete almost felt embarrassed for asking the question. Red chuckled and said, "No, Pete. I gave that up years ago. Bill took over for me and did a great job. I don't miss the traveling. I miss the Garden. And, I do miss aggravating the fans on opposing teams when I'd light up one of these", holding up his cigar, "But, mostly, I miss the guys."

Looking up at the ceiling, his eyes followed the fading trail of cigar smoke. "I remember when I turned 75, the Celtics' organization threw me a birthday party. It wasn't a surprise party because that may have shocked my heart, too much. But it was a good party. Forty-five former players showed up. I was so surprised and humbled. These guys had a lot of other responsibilities, yet they came and spent time with me. And, when I turned 80, guess who came and wished me a happy birthday? Wilt Chamberlin. I can't tell you how many times we fought and battled Philadelphia and Los Angeles. It meant a great deal that Wilt would come and celebrate with me."

Pete loved hearing these stories. He sat there listening and smiling. He remembered seeing these players in their prime. Now, he was able to see them through the stories of their coach and the eyes of their mentor.

Pete leaned forward and asked, "Coach Auerbach, how could you be such a fierce competitor and find the comradery and compassion for your team?"

Red took a puff of his Hoyo, looked up at the ceiling, and reflected, "Any team can be fierce and fearless in competition. At the end of the game, it's about winning . . . working together, working hard and working smart. But there is also a family feeling." He took another puff, almost as though he was generating momentum, "Being a part of a family comes with a strong sense of pride, responsibility and loyalty. When someone put on a Celtic's uniform, they became a part of tradition, something worth working for. In order for Celtic Pride to flourish, each and every member of the organization . . . players, coaches, management . . . everyone has to value the team as a whole over individuals that are a part. There is a focus on "we", instead of "me"."

He continued with an impassioned tone, "When we all have that kind of approach, athletes view their stats, no longer concerned about their points per game, but more focused on the outcome of the game. The question is not how many points they scored, but did we win the game."

Red looked at Pete, smiled and nodded his head, just once and sat back in his chair while taking another puff.

After a few brief moments of contemplative silence, Coach looked at Pete making eye contact, took a puff on his cigar as if to break the silence, and said, "Tell me about your team, Pete. Do you run this show by yourself, or are you a player-coach of The Sanctuary?"

"I have some great guys working here", Pete began to articulate his thoughts, "Guys who like cigars and are pretty good with customers. I give them a list of things to do, and they get them done. But to some, it's just a job."

"And, what about you, Pete? How do you feel about this kind of work? Is it your passion . . . or is it just a position?", Red asked.

Those questions caught Pete off guard. He took a puff on his cigar, looked at Coach and said, "Like I said earlier, I love this place and I love the people who are here, employees and guests. There is just so much I can do. There's also so much I need to learn."

Red grinned and said, "Pete, I love your commitment and appreciation for your people. Let me tell the simplest lesson ever shared with me. Do what you do best. And, take pride in what you do. The kind of pride I'm talking about is not the arrogant puffed-up kind; it's just the whole idea of caring . . . fiercely caring."

"And" Coach Auerbach emphasized, "look after your people. We need to put others first. The best way to forget ones' self is to look at the world with attention and love. Look after your people and love your people. That's it."

Pete was listening intently, and Red could sense his commitment to change. Coach had one last thing to say. He took a long puff, blew it out, looked at the smoke and then turned his eyes toward Pete.

Red, with a tone of commanding and tender authority said, "Coming alongside of others is a high calling in life. Some call it coaching. Others call it caring. Both exemplify forgetting self and focusing on other. Some say coaching is about making decisions. True coaching is about making a difference. Dads, teachers, priests, pastors, managers, business owners and yes, even coaches will impact lives. When they do, they change a destiny and make a difference."

Red looked at his cigar and he had smoked it right down to the band. As he removed the Hoyo de Monterrey band, Pete made a request, "Coach, I need to ask a favor." Red nodded in complete agreement. "Could you write two or three words on the back of your cigar band that would remind me of our conversation? That way, your words will always be with me."

Red smiled. The kind of smile at the end of the game when he would light up a cigar to antagonize the opposing team and thrill the fans. Red pulled out a pencil from the left, lower pocket of his plaid green and white sport coat. He turned over the cigar band and wrote.

Red handed the band to Pete. Pete looked at the band and it read, "Make A Difference". Pete looked at Red, and they both smiled and nodded.

Red stood and said it was time for his to leave. Pete raised his hand to slap a "high five". Red looked at him, moved Pete's had to the side and gave him a hug.

As Red gave a tight squeeze, he gently said, "Appreciate you my friend, you are a great coach. Glad you are a part of this team."

Red couldn't see it, but Pete got a tear in his eye. Coach Red Auerbach was looking after Pete. And to Pete, it felt good.

Red looked at his new friend, winked and turned to walk out the plate glass door of The Sanctuary. As his figure softened in the sunlight, he soon vanished. The Coach had left the building.

Pete looked at the Hoyo cigar band, with the words, "Make A Difference". He opened the humidor. Inside were four cigars and two cigar bands. Pete placed the Coach's band on top of the others and respectfully and carefully closed the lid of the humidor.

A humidor made of Mahogany, dark in color with straight grains from the regions of the Congo in Africa. As old as a legacy, withstanding times of poverty and prosperity. Lined with copper, with a rich patina of truth, purity and change. Ornate symbols on each corner made of precious silver, each shaped as an angelic messenger looking up symbolizing hope. And an emblem on top inscribed with the words, "Iron On Iron, Brother To Brother".

Pete looked at the humidor and wondered what was next. Candidly, he was open to anything and anyone who would come through the plate glass door.

As he was deep in reflective thought, he heard it. The glass door was swinging open.

Persistency Of Purpose – The General

Pete turned to the door. The man walking through had his left hand on the handle, pushing the single piece of plate glass open. As the door made the familiar clicking sound when open, Pete began to discern the eclipsing figure of the person.

The man walked with a deliberate stride. Commanding. Respectful. And authoritative. All his clothing seemed to be dark, although some of that may have been the shadow caused by the light behind him. He wore a coat that was long, almost down to his knees. The coat seemed to be adorned with shiny buttons up and down both sides, as well as some type of filagree on each shoulder. The bottoms of his trousers were tucked inside tall boots. And he wore a hat like an older shaped slouch hat, with a wide flat-top crown.

He wasn't a tall person. Possibly midway between five and six feet. You could tell he was a fit man. His posture was a bit slouched, but very strong and purposeful.

As he got closer, Pete could tell that he had a beard. A very full beard. Not trimmed or shaped. Not long. But, very full as though it had been grown for years yet kept to a shorter length.

And Pete was able to determine that his clothing was military. Old military. Possibly Civil War. If this guy was a re-enactor, he was good. Long officer's jacket, heavy wool vest and trousers, and tall leather boots. The detail and material used in his uniform had a sense of genuineness and authenticity.

As the gentleman stepped closer, it was evident that this new guest had not walked an easy path in life. His eyes were insightful yet wearied. The wrinkles around his face indicated many long days and nights. Yet, he promoted a sense of control and authority.

He stood in the middle of The Sanctuary, hands down by his side. As he looked from one side to the other his eyes locked in with Pete's.

Pete stretched out his hand and said, "Hey, my friend. I'm Pete. Welcome to The Sanctuary. I'm here to make your day great."

With a sense of diplomacy, the man shook Pete's hand. It was a firm handshake, and his hands were rough and callused. "Thank you, sir", the man replied, "My name is Grant. Ulysses Grant."

Pete grinned slightly. "I can't believe this day", he thought guardedly. He didn't want Mr. Grant to feel unwelcomed. Pete continued to shake Grant's hand. "Welcome, sir," Pete said, "I'm sure you've had a long journey. It would be an honor to have you enjoy a cigar in The Sanctuary. Please, sit here." And Pete motioned to the chair that had been occupied by his previous guests.

As Mr. Grant sat in the chair, he removed his slouch hat, placed it on the chair next to him and surveyed the walk-in humidor across from his chair. His eyes followed the shelves of cigars, up and down, then right to left. There were thousands of cigars. Mr. Grant had a look of astonishment on his face. He looked at Pete and said, "Sir, how do you choose a cigar with such numerous offerings?" Pete smiled, "I have that same question every day. I believe I may have a good recommendation for you."

Grant nodded in appreciation while Pete opened Michael's humidor. Inside Pete saw four cigars and three cigar bands. The bands had the words, "Never give up", "Encourage others" and "Make a difference". Pete retrieved the next cigar in line, a Perdomo Habano Bourbon Barrel-Aged Connecticut Epicure. "What a great cigar", Pete thought.

Pete handed the cigar to Mr. Grant. He looked at the cigar, with a slight raise of his eyebrows. He gently slid it under his nose to detect the slight aroma of aged tobacco and he tasted the end of the cigar, detecting a bit of spice. Pete offered to cut the cigar for Mr. Grant, but he declined. The General, with great precision bit off the cap and accurately spit it into the closest Stinky-styled ashtray. Without hesitation, Grant reached into his vest pocket, pulled out long wooden matches and lit his cigar, taking a long, deep draw. He held it in his mouth for a few seconds and then retro-haled the smoke.

Pete smiled, reached in his pocket, and pulled out another cigar. He popped the cap off with his fingernail, lit the cigar with the nearest shop lighter, and took a puff.

Pete looked at this guest and asked, "So, sir. How shall I address you? Mr. Grant? General? Mr. President?" With a kind grin and a hint of humor in his eyes, he said, "Please, sir, call me Ulysses. When men share a cigar, all the formalities are dismissed. We are brothers, iron sharpening iron." Pete appreciated the kindness and was amazed that Mr. Grant used the same phrase that Michael used.

"This is one of the finest cigars I have ever enjoyed", Grant said to Pete, "Where is it from?" "Thank you.", Pete replied. "It's from a family called Perdomo. They are fourth-generation cigar makers that found freedom in this country. This cigar is created using a process called 'bourbon barrel-aged'. The tobaccos are hand-selected and aged for a minimum of six years. The wrappers are from the Connecticut seed and are aged an additional eight months in a bourbon barrel, that has been charred and used to cure bourbon. The result is a cigar full of flavor and complexity, with a hint of bourbon. It may be a cigar that has been crafted for your preferences."

Grant nodded in agreement, took another puff of his cigar and exhaled with a sense of great enjoyment said, "Well, sir, I like the taste of tobacco and I like the taste of bourbon."

Ulysses S. Grant is one of the photos that accents the wall behind the sales area in The Sanctuary. Pete remembered some of the unique and impressive details of Grant's life.

Born Hiram Ulysses Grant in 1822 in Ohio, his father ran a tannery. At the age of seventeen, Grant's father arranged for his son's admission to the U.S. Military Academy at West Point. The congressman who appointed Grant mistakenly believed that his first name was Ulysses, and his middle name was Simpson, his mother's maiden name. The error was never amended, and he went on to accept Ulysses S. Grant as his name.

While at West Point, he was known as an accomplished horseman, but an undistinguished student. After being commissioned as a second lieutenant he saw action in the Mexican-American War. After several unassuming posts with the Army, Grant resigned his commission and began working in his father's business.

After the war between the states began, Grant was commissioned as a colonel with the 21st Illinois Volunteers. In the later part of the summer of 1861, President Lincoln promoted Grant to a brigadier general. Grant's first major victory came the following year in February, when his troops captured Fort Donelson in Tennessee. When inquired about the terms of surrender, Grant replied, "No terms except an unconditional and immediate surrender can be accepted." Following the Battle of Fort Donelson, he became known as "Unconditional Surrender Grant".

The following year, Grant's forces captured Vicksburg. Becoming known as a tenacious, determined and courageous leader, President Lincoln appointed him lieutenant general in 1864 and gave him command of all U.S. armies.

Grant commanded the Union army and after a series of military campaigns, Grant accepted the surrender of General Robert E. Lee at the Appomattox Court House in Virginia in 1865. Five days later, Grant and his wife were scheduled to accompany President and Mrs. Lincoln to the Ford's Theater, the night of the President's assassination. The Grants had to decline due to visiting family. The General had often wondered if could have prevented Booth's assassination of Mr. Lincoln.

President Lincoln said of the General, "The great thing about Grant is his perfect correctness and persistency of power."

Following the war, Grand became a national hero and in 1866 was appointed America's first four-star general at the recommendation of President Andrew Johnson. Three years later, Grant replaced Secretary of War Edwin Stanton, over concerns of a more aggressive approach to Reconstructionism. Eventually, Congress demanded that Stanton be reinstated. In January 1868, Grant resigned his war post. That same month, the Republicans nominated Grant as their presidential candidate.

In the general election, Grant won the electoral college, as well as the popular vote. At the age of 46, he became the youngest president-elect in U.S. history, at that time.

As President, Grant faced challenging times. During Reconstructionism, Southern states were brought back to the Union. President Grant introduced a peaceful reconciliation between the torn North and South. He supported federal pardons for former Confederate leaders while also promoting the protection of civil rights for emancipated slaves. He oversaw the ratification of the 15th Amendment that gave black men the right to vote. Grant approved legislation aimed at limiting the rise of white terrorist that used violence to intimidate.

Grant also signed legislation establishing the Department of Justice, the Weather Bureau and Yellowstone National Park.

He won a second term and began to focus on the ongoing and severe depression that stuck America in 1873.

After leaving office, Grant invested in a financial firm with his son as a partner. Another partner swindled the investors in 1884, causing the business to collapse and bankrupting Grant. To provide for his family, the former general and president decided to write his memoirs, with the help of longtime friend and author, Samuel Clemons, also known as Mark Twain. The successful sales of his story provided substantial income for Grant's family.

History records that Grant died at the age of 63 in 1885. They say that a million people gathered in New York City to witness Grant's funeral processional.

Pete looked over at the chair that other historical heroes had recently occupied and saw an amazing, proven, resilient leader. Grant was simply enjoying his cigar.

"Mr. President," Pete couldn't bring himself to refer to Grant in any other manner, "How's the cigar?"

Grant looked at Pete with a sense of serenity and said, "This is one of more enjoyable pleasures I have experienced. Please tell Mr. Perdomo that he makes an incredible cigar." Pete nodded, smiled and thought, "There's no way that Nick Perdomo would believe this. But it is a great compliment."

"Tell me, sir", Pete continued, "What was it like? A country divided in war. Brother against brother. And is it true that you only extended an unconditional and immediate surrender to those who stood on the other side of battle?"

The General took a puff on his cigar and reflected on Pete's question. It was obvious that Grant had an answer forming. Yet he was strategically choosing the right words to communicate the right message. Even in conversation, Grant was a tactician.

"War is often inevitable". There are always two opposing ideologies. In politics, between countries and domains and even in business. The art of war is simple enough. Find out where your enemy is. Get at him as soon as you can. Strike him as hard as you can and keep moving on." Grant's eyes were focused and his tone calm, but firm.

He continued, "But be assured, sir. I have never advocated war except as a means of peace. Too often, war is a response to tyranny and injustice. There are but few important events in the affairs of men brought about by their own choice." Pete sat in deep thought, listening and trying to capture each and every word.

"Many of the milestones of my life were not on the journey that I had mapped out." Grant paused to take another draw on his cigar. "When a man leads with courage and determination in his personal and professional calling, he will have the opportunity to make choices that benefit his friends, family and fellow citizens. In considering that manday, unconditional surrender is the only option."

"I was educated and commissioned to lead. Once I accepted that calling in my life, I trusted the Almighty to guide me. I have listened to his calling through my superiors and Commander-in-Chief. I have done what I was designed to do." Grant said with a confidence of a proved and tested leader.

"The great general Napoleon Bonaparte said, 'A leader is a dealer in hope'. It has been my mandate to bring about a society and country where all men, no matter their color or creed, find hope."

Pete wished he had a notebook and a pen. How could he remember all of these insightful leadership thoughts? He kept on saying each key point over and over in his head.

The General looked at Pete with a deep inquiring gaze, "Pete, I am enjoying this excellent cigar and your fine company. But why am I here? I have a sense that there is something you may need from me?"

Pete was taken back. In all of the days previous conversations, there was no indication that his previous guests knew they had a specific purpose in coming into The Sanctuary. Was this Grant being the decisive general?

"Well, sir", Pete cautiously continued, "I have led other business leaders and associates for years. During those times, I have had a positive influence, but not an impactful one. I am now the owner of this establishment where men come in everyday to not only enjoy a cigar, but to find a place to belong, a place to converse and a place to call their own. I have been reminded of the principles and practices I have learned in the past but may have forgotten. I need to embrace them, again."

Grant enjoyed a puff, gazed at the billowing smoke and grinned. "Pete, I have learned many things in my life. But many of the lessons that I have learned, I have never fully embraced or lived. A lesson is never learned until it is a lesson lived." Pete sat there in wonder at this simple but significant truth. The General continued, "Aristotle said, 'He who never learned to obey cannot be a good commander'. Following orders is a key to being a good soldier. Following the principles you have learned in the past makes for a good leader."

Pete nodded his head in total agreement. There was a question wrestling in Pete's heart. He needed to ask it, but wasn't confident that the meaning behind the question would be clear.

Pete's eyes fixed on Grant's. He asked, "Mr. President, when are the challenges to great? What if there is too much conflict? Too much work? And it will take too much effort to right the ship?"

Grant paused, looked back at Pete and said with a stern, yet comforting tone, "The great Roman, Publilius Syrus said, 'Anyone can hold the helm when the sea is calm.' I have come to realize that in every battle there comes a time when both sides consider themselves beaten. Then, and only then, he who continues the attack wins. Victory is for the committed. A leader is one who, even when he is fatigued, limited in resources and almost beaten, digs deep within to live the lessons he has learned from others."

Pete sat back in his chair, looked up to ceiling and exhaled. He knew that leading was a act of determination and courage. Both characteristics he must embrace.

Hoping he had shared some encouraging and motivating thoughts, the General leaned forward in his chair, set his cigar on the ashtray, placed his elbows on his knees and clasped his hands together. He looked at Pete and said, "My friend, you must lead yourself before you can lead others. Identify those areas in your life that need improvement and improve them. Read. Journal. Talk with wiser men than you. Learn lessons that you can live and pass to others. A lesson lived is a lesson learned. Be persistent in your purpose. Find courage to stand against foes, fear and failure. When you find this kind of courage, you will lead courageously."

Pete knew that the General had come for a specific reason. And Pete heard the marching orders. Pete looked at Grant and asked, "Sir, may I ask that you leave me with something?" "Anything, Pete", Mr. Grant replied. "I would ask that you take the cigar band off the Perdomo cigar, take this pen and write just two or three words that will remind me of our time together and your insightful words."

Grant nodded. Pete handed him the pen. The General looked at the pen wondering where the inkwell was. Pete smiled and said, "No inkwell needed. Use it like a pencil." Grant looked at it, smiled and wrote the back of the cigar band.

The General who was also a former President stood to his feet, handed the pen and band to Pete and clasped his hands behind his back, as if to stand at ease. As Pete accepted the cigar band, he rose and faced Grant. He turned over the band and read just two words, "Lead Courageously".

The General looked at Pete, with a slight grin which highlighted the deepened wrinkles of war around his eyes and forehead. He reached down to retrieve his slouch hat, placed it on his head and adjusted the brim. He stood in front of Pete and snapped a salute. Pete saluted back.

Without saying another word, Grant turned toward the glass door and began walking out. As Pete's eyes followed, this exit was different than the others. As General Grant was exiting, another figure was entering.

While Grant's stride was purposeful, this other person's stride was playful. Grant's hat was a slouch, this other person's hat was shaped like a Fedora. Grant was dressed in dark navy blue, while this man was dressed in all white.

As they passed, Grant looked at the man and said, "Good day, old friend." And the other man tipped his hat and said, "Good day to you, Mr. President."

Get Going – The Storyteller

As the new guest walked closer to Pete, he was instantly recognizable. His suit was white linen broadcloth from coat to vest to trousers. It was immaculate and crisp as newly fallen snow, as were his neatly pressed white shirt and bow tie. The buttons were covered with the same lined material. And his shoes were a white enameled leather. His hat was a pristine white Fedora, covered his flowing grayish hair. He sported a handlebar-like mustache.

Like many of the pictures Pete had seen in the past and like the one hanging in The Sanctuary, this man was unmistakably Samuel Clemens, or as his many followers knew him, Mark Twain.

Pete walked toward Clemons, stretched out his hand and said, "Hey, my friend. I'm Pete. Welcome to The Sanctuary. I'm here to make your day great."

Clemens firmly grasped Pete's hand quickly offered a warm and welcoming smile and, "Salutations and greetings, sir. It is an extreme pleasure to meet you". And with that, Clemens winked his left eye.

Pete, without wanting to pry said, "I see you had a chance to talk with Mr. Grant." Clemens again smiled, "Yes sir. The President and I go way back. He is a dear friend. Except when you get him on the field of battle." he chuckled. "Many in the nation's capital feel a bit uncomfortable when this southern gentlemen in a white suit steps foot in the White House. I believe they are afraid that I may try to whitewash the fence." Pete laughed and was amazed at the quick humor of Mr. Clemens.

"Well, sir, please come and sit with me for a bit", as Pete motioned to the soft leather chairs sitting in the lounge area. Sam walked over to the hat rack and placed his Fedora on the peg and followed his host. Pete sat in his customary chair with Mr. Clemons to his left, in the same chair used earlier in the day by a Prime Minister, an entertainer, a coach and a former President.

Pete asked, "May I offer you a cigar, sir?" A warm and appreciative smile appeared on Mr. Clemens face. "My friend, that would be the kindest gesture this weary soul could hope for."

Pete slid the humidor closer to his chair. He opened the silver inlaid lid and saw three cigars, as well as four cigar bands. As he surveyed the cigar, he noticed a small Perfecto. He picked it up as if his hand was drawn to it. The cigar was a Fuente Best Seller. Pete looked at the vitola and thought, "This is the perfect cigar for Mark Twain."

Pete handed the Best Seller to Mr. Clemens. He smiled, looked at the size and shape, looked back at Pete, and said, "Very intriguing." Clemens, although a well-known cigar smoker, looked at both ends of the cigar, the foot and head, seemingly wondering which end to cut.

As Pete began to show him the foot of the cigar, Clemens chuckled, "I've got this, young man. This is not my first cigar", he paused, "This is not my first cigar, today." Pete's face reddened with a bit of embarrassment as he tried to instruct one of the greatest humorists, teachers and lecturers in all American culture. Not to mentioned, one of the most noted cigar aficionados of all time.

Clemens popped the cap of the Best Seller with an unusually long pinky fingernail. He placed the cigar in the corner of his mouth, reached into his vest pocket and retrieved a box of long, wooden matches. With the synchronization of a fine-tuned machine, he struck the match, lit his cigar and took a long puff, almost as if in a single motion.

Clemens looked at the billowing smoke and then at the cigar. "For its size, this not yet fully grown cigar is quite a mature and satisfying smoking pleasure." Pete smiled, nodded and thought, "Most people would have said, 'It's good.'"

Pete looked at the Best Seller and was reminded of the family heritage of the Fuente family of cigars. Started in 1912, the Arturo Fuente Cigar Company has impacted the cigar industry with hard work, dedication and tradition. For four generations, the company has remained family owned. Begun by Arturo the Fuente's continue to offer some of the finest Dominican cigars in the world. Carlos, Sr. often said, "We don't hurry things; we just do things the way they are supposed to be done."

The Best Seller is a part of the Hemingway line of the Fuente family. All the shapes are Perfecto, which was very popular during America's golden age. It takes a real master roller to make a true Perfecto cigar. The Best Seller is a Figurado, or a cigar that is rolled without a straight side, in a "figured" shape. Some say that these are cigars rolled with tapers and curves. The Best Seller uses Dominican binder and filler, with a Cameroon wrapper. Although this cigar may be small at four and a half inches in length and a 55-ring gauge at the center of the cigar, it is packed tight with tobacco and flavor. Most find this cigar to be a 45-minute enjoyable smoke.

Samuel Clemens, or as some know him by his pen name, Mark Twain, was an American writer, humorist, entrepreneur, publisher and lecturer. He was acclaimed as the greatest humorist the United States has ever produced. The great author, William Falkner called him, "the father of American literature". His noted works included, "The Adventures of Tom Sawyer", "The Adventures of Huckleberry Finn" and "The Great American Novel". Raised in Hannibal, Missouri he was familiar with the surroundings he would later use as backdrops for his novels. Clemens was renowned for his story telling. His wit and satire, in prose and in speech, earned praise from critics and peers, and he was a friend to presidents, artists, industrialists and European royalty.

As Pete looked over at Mr. Clemens, obviously enjoying his Best Seller, Pete reached in his pocket and pulled out a cigar for his own enjoyment. He asked, "Mr. Clemens, tell me about your friendship with the President?"

Sam smiled, saying, "Well, Pete. There are a great number of people who may pay me great sums of money to know all the familiarities of my friendship with Ulysses S. Grant. He is a great leader and a compassionate President. It is uncommon to find the delicate balance between soldier and statesman. Mr. Grant has found that balance. He is a friend for which I would give my livelihood and my life." Clemens paused and with a serious and gentle humorous tone said, "The trouble is not in dying for a friend, but in finding a friend worth dying for. I have found that in Mr. Grant."

Pete sensed that his time with Clemens would be limited. Each of his previous visitors stayed for the amount of time it took to smoke their cigar. Clemens had a Best Seller and seemed to be a very passionate and aggressive cigar smoker.

Pete decided to be forthright in his conversation with Clemens. He said, "Mr. Clemens.", Clemens gently raised his hand motioning for Pete to stop. Clemens said, "Pete, if we are going to talk about friends, we will probably become friends. Over the years, I have found that it is particularly pleasing if my friends call me Sam. So, please call me Sam. That is if you want to be my friend?" Sam smiled with his whole face.

Pete smiled and nodded, "Thank you, Sam. You are one of most beloved humorists and authors in American history. Your writings are timeless, filled with warmth and humor, yet they are relevant to the culture of the day. Many of the lessons from years ago are still applicable today." Sam nodded in appreciation. "How did you do it? How did you get started?"

Sam took a long draw on this Best Seller. He looked at Pete and said, "Well, my friend. Although I didn't know we were going to engage in such meaningful dialogue, I rather enjoy talking about myself." Pete smiled, knowing that Samuel's comment had an element of truth.

Sam said, "The secret of getting ahead is getting started. The secret of get started is breaking your complex and overwhelming tasks into small manageable tasks and starting on the first one. Whatever the story, the lecture or the assignment, I found that I needed to start the process by looking at the pieces, starting to accomplish small tasks and putting them together into a larger completed work."

Pete nodded. "Too often", Sam continued, "our own unresponsiveness to challenges causes us to be paralyzed to the steps needed to move forward. If we accept responsibility for our ideas and our actions, we can take the first step on the journey of fulfillment. Don't wait for others to give you the solutions, needed. Find them yourself. They are your hidden treasure ready for you to discover."

Pete leaned in and said, "Sam, there have been times when I thought my ambitions and dreams were unattainable. The hardest part is when others think the same thing."

Sam paused Pete and said, "My friend, keep away from people who try to belittle your dreams, ideas and ambitions. These are small people who are intimidated by your big ideas. Small people always do that, but the really great ones make you feel that you, too, can become great. That is why I appreciate my President. He believes that others can be great. Whether they are black or white, poor or rich, common or prestigious, a good author or a struggling writer, we all have an opportunity for greatness if we take the bull by the horns and accept responsibility. Just one caution, make sure you hang on tight to the bull's horns."

Sam smiled with a whimsical and wise smile, "Twenty years from now you will be more disappointed by the things that you didn't do than by the ones that you did do. So, throw off the bowlines. Sail away from the safe harbor. Catch the trade winds in your sails." Each sentence. Each word became more impassioned. "Explore. Dream. Discover." Sam was pointing at Pete to emphasize each word.

Pete sat back in his chair, took a puff on his cigar, blew out the smoke and said, "That's a great deal to think about."

Sam leaned forward, placed his cigar in his left hand, and using both arms in a wide, expansive gesture said, "Pete, the two most important days in your life are the day you born and the day you find out why." Sam leaned back, took a puff on his cigar and said, "Now, that was a good thought", chuckling at his own wit and insights.

Pete, processing all that Sam had said, looked at him with an inquisitive stare. "Sam," he said, "would it be inappropriate if I asked how old you are?" Sam looked at him and spoke with the timing of a great comedian, "How old am I? My friend, I quit having birthdays years ago. I'm dead. In fact, Pete, all your guests today have passed on. We are all here for you."

For the first time, Pete had a sense of relief, as well as concern. Sam's comment gave some insight into those who had been visiting The Sanctuary, but there were still some unanswered questions. Was Pete also dead? Was this part of eternity. Was he in a coma due to a head injury? All the questions quickly ceased when Sam spoke.

"Pete, trust me, friend. This will all make sense, soon." His words were calculated, but not reassuring. "Accept responsibility for what took place earlier, for what you have experienced today, and for what will come," Sam said in a calming and instructive tone.

"Every day we are presented with opportunity and opposition. Faith allows us to see and embrace the opportunity. Fear hinders us when we succumb to and envision the fear. Choose faith and combat fear. One will release you to accomplish all that you were created and gifted to do. The other will atrophy your hopes and dreams. Evaluate the opportunities that are before you. With each opportunity comes a new responsibility. Accept responsibility."

Pete nodded with a deep sense of appreciation. He looked at Sam and asked, "Sir, as you may know, I would like to remember the things that you have told me today. Would you be willing to write two or three . . .". Mr. Clemens gently raised his right hand as motioning Pete to stop talking. He reached into his pocket and pulled out a well used pencil, removed the band from the Arturo Fuente Best Seller, turned it over, licked the end of the pencil and wrote the words, "Accept Responsibility". He handed it to Pete and said, "So, my friend, what are you going to do with my cigar band? You know, it could be a best seller."

Pete smiled and reached over to the humidor presented to him by Michael. As he opened this lid, place the cigar band with the words, "Accept Responsibility" on top of the other four bands. Sam said, "Next time, you're going to have to tell me the story about the humidor."

A humidor made of Mahogany, dark in color with straight grains from the regions of the Congo in Africa. As old as a legacy, withstanding times of poverty and prosperity. Lined with copper, with a rich patina of truth, purity and change. Ornate symbols on each corner made of precious silver, each shaped as an angelic messenger looking up symbolizing hope. And an emblem on top inscribed with the words, "Iron On Iron, Brother To Brother".

Both gentlemen stood, now deeply committed friends, and shook hands. Pete asked, "How is this going to end?" Sam responded with a reassuring tone in his voice, "Like all great stories. With a happy ending."

Samuel Clemens nodded and winked, almost in one motion. Turned toward the plate glass door, retrieved his white Fedora, placed it on his head with a slight adjustment, and walked out of The Sanctuary.

As his familiar silhouette faded in the bright lights coming through the glass, Pete turned and started his normal routine of wiping down the coffee tables and cleaning the ashtrays. Although today, there were just two ashtrays. Pete's ashtray and the one where his special guests sat.

Not knowing where this day would end, Pete continued to reflect on the wisdom and insights he had heard throughout the day. "Never give up", "Encourage others", "Make a difference", "Lead courageously", and "Accept responsibility". These simple statements were all filled with truth. Truth that could turnaround a life . . . or a business.

Be Open Handed – The Pastor

It occurred to Pete that the only customers he had today were not his normal guests. But only the special guests. He looked at this watch and it seemed is if time had not moved. Pete could recall the moments he spent with each person . . . Michael, the Prime Minister, Gracie's guy, the Coach, Mr. President and Mark Twain . . . moments had passed but time had not moved.

Pete finished cleaning, although it did not take much time. He arranged the ashtrays, cutters and lighters on the coffee tables, so they were accessible to each guest, no matter where they sat. He looked around and thought, "This is good". He then slapped the cleaning cloth on his hand as if to announce that his work was done.

As Pete began to walk past the door to the walk-in humidor, around the chairs of eight and to the back of the shop near the sales area, he looked up to the wall of photographs. In neat columns and rows were images of famous cigar aficionados throughout history. Some were well known, and some were not. There were politicians, entertainers, sports figures, authors, business tycoons, and even a preacher.

In the middle of all these famous people that were recognizable, there was another photograph. Not famous to many people but known to those in The Sanctuary. It was a picture of Pap.

Pap, whose given name was "Robert", and some called him "Bob", was a long timer in the family of The Sanctuary. He often worked during the day. He was one of those people with whom guests would comfortably sit down and converse. Pap had a wealth of knowledge on subjects. Well, let's say he knew a little about a lot. Except for two topics . . . baseball and the Bible.

Pap was an avid Yankee's fan. He knew statistics and players from the golden era of baseball. He knew who he liked and who he didn't like. Pap was Babe Ruth blue, through and through. The picture on the wall, surrounded by celebrities, showed Pap wearing a Yankees hat and a pin striped baseball jersey, smoking a cigar.

Before becoming a part of The Sanctuary, Bob had several career accomplishments. He owned a sporting goods store, managed a shooting preserve and was a preacher. Many guests didn't know Pap was a pastor. In his prime years, Bob started a church in the northeast. He grew the church with his skill as a preacher and orator. His Sunday sermons were down to earth and practical. He knew the Bible and could quote verses from memory.

When men, of all ages, young and old, would sit in The Sanctuary, light up a cigar and needed to talk, Pap was there with not only a listening ear, but often life-changing insights and advice. He was always encouraging and instructive. Pap would often say "God plants the seeds of grace in a man's heart. I just help get the soil ready."

Pete gazed at Pap's picture; in the middle of celebrities, wearing a Yankee's hat and pinstripes, and smoking a cigar, and thought how famous Bob was to the everyday guests to The Sanctuary.

As Pete was reminiscing, he heard the plate glass door of The Sanctuary open on its decade old hinges. He turned and again was only able to see an outline of a short statured man. He walked in with a sense of authority. As he walked closer, Pete could tell this gentleman was from a time in the past. He was dressed in a 19th Century style suite, dark and layered with heavy cloth. His shirt was billowing out near the neck and his tie was like a thick ribbon. He wore a short, stovepipe black hat. Although purposeful in his stride, the man walked with a slight hesitation, causing him to use a thin, black cane with a silver grip. As Pete was able to recognize the gentleman's features, he saw boyish features in his face, yet a heavy beard with long, raven-like hair billowing from under his hat.

Pete slowly moved toward the guest and said, "Hello, my friend. I'm Pete. Welcome to The Sanctuary. I'm here to make your day great."

The gentleman nodded in acknowledgement of Pete's greeting, removed his hat, offered his hand and said, in a clear, almost trumpet like voice, "Thank you, kind sir. My name is Charles. Charles Hadden Spurgeon."

Although many may not know the name, Pete did. As an avid reader, he had come across Spurgeon's writings or commentaries on the Holy Scriptures. Spurgeon had published a volume called, "Lectures To My Students", which included twenty-eight lectures to young men who sensed a call to serve others.

"Mr. Spurgeon", Pete said, "I'm honored to have you here at The Sanctuary." "The Sanctuary?", Spurgeon replied, "What an appropriate name for an establishment that promotes and supplies the wonderful gift of cigars."

Pete motioned for Spurgeon to sit in the lounge area, in the same seat that others before him had occupied. As Mr. Spurgeon hung his hat on the rack, he resolutely walked over to the comfortable leather chair, used his cane to help secure his seat and sat with a sigh of enjoyment. "Very comfortable, sir. I have a sense that many great men before me have occupied this seat", he said. As he sat in his chair, Pete thought, if he only knew.

As Mr. Spurgeon rested his cane against his chair, surveyed the shop he smiled and nodded in approval. Pete said, "Sir, it would be an honor to share a cigar. May I offer you one?" Spurgeon smiled and said, "My good man, the gift of a cigar is one of the most generous and gratuitous gestures a brother of the leaf can make. It would be my honor to accept such a gift."

Pete leaned forward in his chair, reverently took hold of the prized humidor sitting on the coffee table and slid it toward him. As he opened the lid, he saw just two cigars and five cigar bands. Pete reached for the next cigar in line and offered it to Mr. Spurgeon. The cigar was a Monte Cristo White Series.

Mr. Spurgeon accepted the cigar with two hands as if receiving a prized treasure. He carefully studied the cigar, examining the foot and head, sniffing the foot and thoughtfully considering all its lines. He looked at Pete in approval.

Pete offered to cut and light the cigar for Mr. Spurgeon. With the careful precision of a cigar sommelier, Pete used a cutter to make a V-cut. He made two cuts. One north and south, and the other east and west. The cuts formed a cross. He then gently toasted the foot of the cigar and then handed it to his guest. Without hesitation, Mr. Spurgeon brought the cigar to his mouth as Pete continued to offer the flame. The theologian took several continuous puffs to fully ignite the cigar. As he sat back in his chair, with a sense of satisfaction, he took a long puff, sighed and said, "This is an aromatic sensation. Thank you, sir."

"Tell me about this cigar, sir. I am unfamiliar with its origin and profile."

Pete pulled a cigar from one of the stragglers in his pocket, cut and lit with swiftness. After taking his first puff, Pete said, "The Monte Cristo White Series is one of the most sought-after cigars. It has Dominican and Nicaraguan long leaf fillers, a Nicaraguan binder and wrapped with a Connecticut seed Ecuadorian shade leaf. Many say it is smooth and full of flavor. This cigar produces a generous amount of smoke and aroma. The name Monte Cristo means 'Mountain of Christ' in Spanish".

"Thank you, Pete. May I call you Pete?", said Mr. Spurgeon. "Of course, sir", he replied. "And, please call me Charles. Your gift of this cigar has established a friendship by which we can use given names. 'Mountain of Christ'? I am very fond of that name." Charles paused in thought, nodded and enjoyed another long puff.

"I had stated on several occasions that I intend to smoke a good cigar to the glory of God before I go to bed. This is a good cigar and to God be the glory", Spurgeon playfully said.

Charles inquired, "I have another question, Pete. I hope I am not an inconvenience. Please take a moment and tell me the story of this beautiful humidor." Pete smiled and shared the story of Michael, his account of growing up and the significance of the humidor. Pete talked about the precious material used to make the humidor, the meaning of the emblem and the significance of such a great gift.

Charles had taken several puffs from his cigar, nodding in approval as Pete related the story. Charles said, "Pete, I'm not sure you may know the origination of Michael's name. It means, 'Gift from God'." Charles continued, "This humidor is truly a gift to you from the hand of God."

Pete looked up, with emotion on his face, and slowly nodded in agreement. After a moment, Pete asked Charles, "What does my name mean?" With a slight grin, Charles took another puff on his cigar. He simply said, "Rock. You are the rock upon which The Sanctuary is built."

As both men sat back in their chairs and enjoyed cigars, Pete was deep in thought. Looking over at his guest, he recalled some of the facts he remembered about Charles Hadden Spurgeon.

Spurgeon was known as the "Prince of Preachers" during the mid-1800's in London. Born in 1834 in Kelvedon, Essex, England he made a profession to follow Christ at a young age, hearing the words from the Old Testament prophet Isaiah, "Look unto me, and be ye saved, all the ends of the earth, for I am God, and there is none else." He preached his first sermon at the age of 16. The next year, he was installed as pastor of a small church in Waterbeach, Cambridgeshire.

At 19 years of age, he was called to the pastorate of London's famed New Park Street Chapel in Southwark. At the time, it was the largest Baptist congregation in London. Within a few months, he was asked to shepherd Park Street church, which in later years became Metropolitan Tabernacle. While at Metropolitan Temple, he built Almshouse, a center to care for the homeless and disadvantaged, and Stockwell Orphanage.

He is said to have produced powerful sermons of penetrating thought and defined exposition. His oratory skills held listeners on the edge of their seats while piercing their hearts.

In 1856, Spurgeon was speaking at the Surrey Gardens Music Hall. Someone in the crown yelled, "Fire!" The resulting panic and stampeding crowd left several dead. Spurgeon was emotionally devastated by the sobering event. For many years following, he spoke of being moved to tears at the remembrance of that evening.

In 1857, Spurgeon spoke to the largest crowd ever consisting of over 23,000 people. Spurgeon noted, "A day or two before preaching at the Crystal Palace, I went to decide where the platform should be fixed; and in order to test the acoustic properties of the building, cried in a loud voice, 'Behold the Lamb of God, which taketh away the sin of the world.'"

"In one of the galleries, a workman, who knew nothing of what was being done, heard the words, and they came like a message from heaven to his soul. He was smitten with conviction, put down his tools, went home, and there, after a season of spiritual struggle, found peace and life by beholding the Lamb of God."

In the spring of 1861, the Park Street Church relocated and built the Metropolitan Tabernacle at Elephant and Castle in Southwark, seating 5,000 parishioners, with standing room for another 1,000. Spurgeon would speak several times a week to thousands of people.

During his pastorship, Spurgeon was strongly opposed to the owning of slaves. He wrote, "Not so very long ago our nation tolerated slavery in our colonies. Philanthropists endeavored to destroy slavery; but when it was utterly abolished? It was when the church of God was aroused and addressed herself to the conflict, then she tore the evil thing to pieces. I do from my inmost soul detest slavery. And I will commune at the Lord's table with men of all creeds, yet with a slaveholder I have no fellowship of any sort or kind."

Spurgeon had a history of ailments, including the onset of gout at the age of 33. Spurgeon died at the age of 57, from chronic gout and congestion of the kidneys.

From the fall of 1891 until his death in February 1892, he received 10,000 "letters of condolence, resolutions of sympathy and telegrams of enquiry."

On the day of his funeral, eight hundred extra police were on duty for the cortege. There were sixty-five pair-horse broughams, almost three hundred private carriages which estimated nearly two miles in length for the processional. An estimated 100,000 people passed by Spurgeon as he lay in state or attended the funeral, with an unknown number lining the streets.

There are no audio recordings of Spurgeon, so his voice can no longer be heard. Yet, without amplification, his voice; with clarity, command and passion reached thousands each week. His sermons were said to be theologically precise, culturally relevant, convicting to the heart and focused on the Savior.

By the time of his death in 1892, Spurgeon had preached nearly 3,600 sermons and published 49 volumes of commentaries, sayings, anecdotes, poetry, hymns, illustrations and devotions.

Pete looked over at Charles, knowing that this man was one of a kind, a unique and gifted communicator, who shook the 19th century with his teaching and passion for the Almighty.

As Pete considered this, he had a new sense and freedom in talking with his guests. Samuel Clemens indicated to Pete that all of the day's guests had passed on. They were no longer of this world. Pete still wasn't sure how to think about all of this, but he did have the liberty to talk with Charles with frankness and candor.

Pete asked, "Charles, I appreciate your visit today. Is there a reason that you have stopped by The Sanctuary?"

Charles smiled, "Well. My friend, this is a wonderful haven for the weary soul. It is not only welcoming, but the hospitality is inviting. If I were to consider my reason for being with you today, I would confess that I am here to encourage you and to challenge you."

Pete thought for a moment, "You visiting The Sanctuary is an encouragement to me, as well as all of the other guest, today." Charles nodded as he was aware of the other guests. "How can you challenge me today?"

"You are an extremely gifted shopkeeper and conversationalist, Pete. These are your talents, likely bestowed on you by the Almighty. Give an account of your stewardship as to your talents." Charles continued, "We all vary in natural gifts and skills. One person has the tongue of eloquence, another the pen of a ready writer, and a third the artistic eye that discerns beauty; but whichever of these we may have, they belong to God and ought to be used in His service. All that you do in The Sanctuary draws men to a recognition of who they truly are and why they have been created."

Pete was beginning to see his unique skills and talents, and how they impacted those who were his customers . . . his regular, living customers.

Charles took a long puff on his cigar, looked intently at Pete, and with a clarion tone in his voice he said, "My dear Pete, I once heard a man say, 'Nothing you have is yours. It was given to you by God, so hold it loosely.' I have tried to live out this precept, in all areas of my life, not just ministry." Pete wondered if there were parts of his business that he held too tight in his grip.

"I have tried to live with an open hand", Charles said, while illustrating with his hand. "When God places something in my hand, I am presented with two opportunities. The first is to clench my hand and claim what has been placed within. The second is to leave it open. If I clench the item within, it will always be mine. If the same item is left in an open hand, God can take it out as He pleases, and replace it with what He wishes. This is living with an open hand."

As Charles was talking, Pete was looking at this hand. Had he held on to The Sanctuary so tightly that he impeded its growth and innovation?

Charles could sense that Pete was trying to sort some things out in his heart. With the eyes of tender and compassionate pastor, Charles said, "Pete, what are you doing with all the has been entrusted to you? Is it yours to keep or is it yours to give"?

Pete sat there with a sense of conviction. He had told others that The Sanctuary was simply that, a sanctuary. He looked at Charles and said, "This place . . . this cigar shop is truly a sanctuary. It is a refuge and shelter for men to find their purpose and meaning in life. It was a place for younger men to be encouraged by sage, older men. It was a place where men are accepted, challenged and motivated to reach higher and to run life's race with resilience." Pete had never really articulated those words before.

Charles looked at him in affirmation and assurance. "That my friend, is embracing eternity. That is envisioning the tomorrow for men who may have faltered in their yesterday. That ushers in hope for the hopeless and triumph for the downtrodden." Charles paused and then with great deliberation said, "There is a verse of wisdom that illustrates your conviction, Pete. It's found in the writings of King Solomon and recorded as one of his wise proverbs, 'Iron sharpens iron, so a man sharpeneth the countenance of his friend.'"

Pete felt energized. He remembered the phrase that Michael used when talking about the humidor, "Iron on Iron, Brother to Brother". He seemed to have a renewed sense of direction. As he continued to consider these concepts, he began doubting that he had the ability to do all of this. His faith was wavering.

Pete looked at Charles with a sense of fear, "I don't know if I can do this. I'm not sure I have the faith or courage to pull this off."

The wise and compassionate pastor focused his eyes on Pete's and said, "Faith is believing that Christ is what He is said to be, and that He will do what He has promised to do, and then to expect this of Him. If God has put this in your heart to accomplish, He will give you the heart to achieve it."

Pete was moved. He sensed that something was stirring in his heart. And Charles could see it also.

"Pete", Charles said in a reassuring tone, "It is not great faith, but true faith, that saves; and the salvation lies not in the faith, but in the Christ in whom faith trusts. It is not the measure of faith, but the sincerity of faith, which is the point to be considered."

Pete felt a sense of ease. He briefly lowered his head in a moment of silence and dedication.

Charles asked, "Are you good, my friend?" Pete answered, "Yes. I'm sensing that my handling of this business will require faith. But also there is a measure of faith that is needed in my life."

"Yes, Pete", Charles said in a reassuring tenor, "That part is the Almighty's concern, not mine." And then Charles took another puff of his cigar, with a slight smile on the corners of his mouth, somewhat hidden by his beard.

Charles said, "Pete, plan for your everyday, but push for eternity. One is temporary, while the other is permanent. One will vanish, the other will last. One will bring riches and rewards on this earth, the other will bring riches and reward in the heavenlies. Invest in others. Discern deceit. Live wisely. Show mercy. Give grace. Embrace eternity."

Charles Hadden Spurgeon placed his Monte Cristo cigar on the ashtray, leaned forward in his chair, placed his hands on Pete's shoulders and asked the Almighty God to bless him. Pete was moved and held back the tears.

As soon as Charles was done praying, he firmly, but gently slapped both of Pete's shoulders and said, "My dear friend, Pete. It is time for me to leave this harbor of hope and sail on to my next assignment."

Pete placed his hands on Charles' hands, still on his shoulder and said, "Thank you, pastor." And Charles nodded in agreement and gratitude.

Pete had one last request, "Charles, if I am like many of those who heard your messages, I will most likely have a difficult time remembering all that you shared with me. As with all of my previous guests, I have asked them to remove their cigar bands and write two or three words to memorialize their words of encouragement. Would you be so kind?"

Charles smiled. Removed the band from the Monte Cristo White Series, turned it over, retrieved a pencil from his coat pocket and wrote the words, "Embrace Eternity".

He then took the band, placed it in both hands and presented it to Pete. Pete smiled, nodded his head in appreciation and accepted the Monte Cristo White Series band.

Both men stood. Charles picked up his cane from its resting place next to his chair, slowly walked over to the door, place his hat on his full head of black hair and slightly tipped the brim. He smiled and walked to the plate glass door. As he left, Pete could hear Charles humming a hymn.

As he opened the glass door, the familiar clicking sound notified Pete that the door had been used. Charles image quickly faded. He had moved on.

Pete looked at the words, "Embrace Eternity". It felt as if he did. He slowly walked over to his chair, sat down, open the lid and placed the Monte Cristo's band in the humidor.

A humidor made of Mahogany, dark in color with straight grains from the regions of the Congo in Africa. As old as a legacy, withstanding times of poverty and prosperity. Lined with copper, with a rich patina of truth, purity and change. Ornate symbols on each corner made of precious silver, each shaped as an angelic messenger looking up symbolizing hope. And an emblem on top inscribed with the words, "Iron On Iron, Brother To Brother".

Fight Your Fear – The Champ

Pete stared at the inside of the humidor. There was one cigar remaining. Who was it for? Would there be another guest to walk through the door of The Sanctuary?

There were also six cigar bands, each with a truth written on the back that had the influence to turn thoughts and lives around.

Pete respectfully examined each one. The band from the Ashton Prime Minister with the words, "Never Give Up"; the band from El Producto Queens read, "Encourage Others"; the band from the Hoyo de Monterrey had three words, "Make A Difference"; Grant's Perdomo Bourbon Barrell Aged Connecticut cigar band simply read, "Lead Courageously"; the band from the Fuente Best Seller had the words, "Accept Responsibility; and the band from Mr. Spurgeon's Monte Cristo White Series read, "Embrace Eternity".

He placed them back into the humidor, in the exact same order. Each one with a profound truth. Each one in its place.

As Pete closed the lid of the humidor, he heard that familiar clicking sound of the front glass door swinging on the hinge. He stood, knowing that a guest was coming in, and walked toward the entrance of The Sanctuary.

The light was still bright, although it seemed later in the day. A large shadow entered. The darkened outline filled the entire door. Where almost all the other guests had a short stature, this person did not.

Close to six feet tall, and probably two hundred plus in pounds. Pete could tell it was an athletic and fit man. His shoulders were broad and muscular. His arms indicated that he had spent many years building strength and power. His entire upper body symbolized strength. As he walked in, there was a swagger of confidence and domination. His stride had a sense of determined intimidation. As he moved closer, Pete could tell that he was a very dark-skinned man. His hair was closely cropped, and his face was that of a warrior. Focused. Steely. Intent. Powerful.

He was wearing simple clothes. A running suit and athletic shoes. The running suit was black with a white, round neck t-shirt, and the shoes were white, with a heavy sole.

Pete met him just near the door to the walk-in humidor, next to the Cigar Indian and near the seating area, "Hello, my friend. I'm Pete. Welcome to The Sanctuary. I'm here to make your day great."

The man looked at Pete, without a change in his expression. He said, "Thanks, man. My name is Joe. Some call me 'Smokin' Joe'. I'm Joe Frazier."

Pete reached out his hand to welcome his guest. Joe's hands were huge, strong, hard as a rock and callused. His grip was firm . . . very firm. Pete said, "Good to meet you, Champ. Glad you're here. Can I offer you a cigar?" Joe nodded in agreement, Pete motioned him over to the seating area and the chair that had been occupied by six other guests.

Joe said, "Thank you, brother", and plopped in the chair, adjusting his weight and sinking into the soft and luxurious leather.

As Pete opened the lid of the humidor sitting on the coffee table, he asked, "Joe, do you smoke many cigars?" Pete didn't know. Joe Frazier was known as a casual cigar guy. Joe looked up from admiring the leather chair, "No. I have an occasional cigar. But I enjoy them. A lot of folks think because I'm called 'Smokin Joe', it's because I smoke a lot. Nope. That ain't right. I'm called 'Smokin Joe' because I'm like a freight train when it comes to fighting. My manager, Yank gave me the name. It stuck. But I do enjoy a cigar."

As Pete picked the last cigar in the humidor, he handed it to Joe. "What is it?" said Joe. Pete hadn't noticed, but the cigar was a perfect selection. Pete said, "That cigar, my friend, is called the Kristoff Vengeance." Joe smiled, "I like that. Retribution. Punishment. Vengeance. Yep. That's a good cigar for me."

Pete could tell that Joe had smoked some cigars, but he was not a lover of cigars. Pete offered to cut Joe's cigar. He asked if Joe wanted a V-cut, straight cut or punch. Without hesitation, Joe said punch.

Joe admired the clean hole that had been created at the head of the cigar. He picked up a table lighter and clicked it several times. The lighter would ignite, but not stay lit. Pete looked and shook his head. He apologized to Joe, "Hey man, I'm sorry. Every cigar shop has a problem keeping lighters going. You can buy expensive ones or cheap ones. It doesn't matter. Eventually they all start giving you trouble." Pete reached over and grabbed a single-flame torch and handed it to Joe. Joe showed a bit of skill in toasting the end of the cigar, lighting the foot and taking several puffs. As Pete watched in approval, he grabbed a cigar from his pocket. It was the last one he had.

"Tell me about this cigar", Joe said. "It's great!" Pete smiled and replied, "It's an excellent cigar, made by Kristoff Cigars. It has Nicaraguan and Dominican filler, with a Indonesian binder which holds all of the long leaf in place. The wrapper is a Connecticut Broadleaf. This cigar smokes with a rich flavor and should be medium to full bodied in strength. This is an excellent cigar and lives up to its name."

Joe took another puff, blew out the smoke, and looked at the rich and dark wrapper. "I like this. It's got a good taste and feel. Vengeance? I like it." He took another puff in approval and exhaled the smoke.

Pete remembered Joe Frazier as a boxer and World Champion. But he was not familiar with his early life or career. Pete took a puff on his cigar and said, "Joe, tell me about yourself. Where did you grow up and how did you get into boxing?"

Joe looked toward the ceiling and smiled. It wasn't a big, toothy smile. It was a reminiscing smile.

"Well, I was born in Beaufort, South Carolina. I was the twelfth child in my family. Although they named me Joe, my daddy used to call me "Billy Boy", after a Ford car. My daddy, Rubin, had to have his left hand and part of his forearm amputated after some guy shot him over a girlfriend. Think of that." Joe continued, "When I was young, my family had a hog. Well, one day that hog started chasing me. I fell and broke my left arm. They set it to heal, but they didn't set it right. For the rest of my life, even into boxing, my left arm was crooked, and I never had a full range of motion. Didn't seem to matter much, though."

Joe took another puff on his cigar, followed the smoke with his eyes and said, "I remember when Daddy bought a black and white television. We were excited. All my brothers and sisters would sit around and watch boxing matches. Dad would invite the neighbors over and mother would sell drinks for a quarter. We would watch Sugar Ray Robinson, Rocky Marciano, Willie Pep and Rocky Graziano. One night my Uncle Israel noticed a boy with a stocky build boxing. Uncle Israel said that boy could be the next 'Joe Louis'. I thought that boy could be me. The next day, I found an old burlap bag, filled it with rags, corncobs, Spanish Moss and a couple of bricks. I hung that bag in the backyard off an old tree and every day, for six or seven years, would hit that bag. I'd warp my hands in daddy's old necktie and get to it. Oh man, I would hit it hard. That's when I started dreaming about boxing."

"I left home and moved to Philadelphia when I was a teenager. I worked in a slaughterhouse and accidently sliced off the tip of my left pinky with a butcher's knife. So, that's my crooked left arm and my shortened left pinky finger. How about that?" Joe chuckled.

"I started boxing at a local gym. Some of the older men would give me some coaching and teach me some basic skills and techniques. I was big and strong, from all the hard work on the farm in South Carolina and the butchery in Philly."

"One of the men who gave me pointers always said, 'Joe, you got to take what's in front of you. When it gets tough, you gonna want to sit back and be passive. That's when you gotta dig deep and be strong. With all you got, resist being passive, find your purpose and be powerful.' I never forgot that . . . resist being passive. It was up to me to 'flip the switch' in my head. Passive or passion? I decided to be passionate about boxing and tapped into my power. In the early 1960's, the trainers in my gym entered me into the Golden Gloves tournament as a heavyweight. I won in 1962, 1963 and 1964."

Joe continued, "I made the 1964 Olympic team as an alternate. I didn't have to go to Tokyo, but I wanted. While there, I worked out and sparred with anyone who wanted to train. In my head, I heard that old man from Philly say, 'Resist passivity.' So, I took them all on. Middleweight, Light Heavyweight, it didn't matter. I just wanted to fight. Buster Mathis, the heavyweight representative for the United States, got injured, so I got the chance to step up and compete."

"I knocked out George Oywello from Uganda in the first round. Then, I knocked out Athol McQueen from Australia in the third round," Joe's voice was getting louder and intense.

"In the semi-final, I was set to face Vadim Yemelyanov of the Soviet Union. My left hook was doing damage. He couldn't get away from it. Twice in the second round, I knocked him to the canvas. But as I pounded away, I felt a pain shoot through my left arm. It was the thumb on my left hand. I had damaged it. But I had to go on. The adrenaline kicked in and I was ready to continue, no matter what. With just under a minute in the second round, the Soviet's manager threw in the towel. Yemelyanov was done and I was on to the Gold Medal round."

Pete had never heard this story before and he was on the edge of his seat, smoking very quickly.

Joe continued with a look of grimace and pain, even though the match was years ago, "I was facing the German Hans Huber. He was a big guy and eight years older than me. I had to push through the pain and go at him. I couldn't be passive in any manner. In my mind, I kept on saying, 'Resist passivity. Resist passivity. Be aggressive and resist being passive.' When the opening bell rang, I started throwing punches, mostly right-handed, which threw off Huber. Once in a while I would land a left. At the end of the fight, I had won by decision, 3-2. I was a Gold Medal Olympian."

Joe took a puff on his cigar and once again, followed the smoke.

"Joe, tell me about becoming World Champion. And would you tell me about Ali?" Pete asked.

Joe shook his head, not in a negative way, but in a frustrating way. "Ali. Everybody wants to know about Ali".

Taking a puff on the Vengeance, Joe began, "My trainer, Yank Durham, helped put together some businessmen who invested in my pro career. In the mid-1960's, I turned pro. My first year, I won all my fights by knockouts. In the late part of 1965, I injured my eye in a training accident. I was legally blind but didn't tell anybody. When I had an eye exam, I would cover the same eye with different hands. The doc never knew the difference."

"I continued to fight and win, usually by knockout. In February 1967, I had 14 wins, and I was starting to get noticed. That's the month I met Ali. At that point, the guy was the World Heavyweight Champion. Later that year, Ali was stripped of his title because he refused to serve in the military. To fill the vacant title, the New York State Athletic Association held a fight between me and Buster Mathis . . . ole' Buster. I knocked him out in the 11th round and became Heavyweight Champion."

"In 1971, Ali and I fought in the Garden for the first time. It was called the 'Fight of the Century'. Ali was tough. But I was tougher. Any passivity would be seen as a weakness. I had to be smart. I had to be strong. I had to be strategic. Ali won the first two rounds. I got better in the middle rounds. I hammered his body and got some great left hooks in to his head. At the end of the night, I won by unanimous decision from all three judges. It was the best night in my life."

"In 1973, Yank passed away and Eddie Futch became my trainer. I can't tell you how many times I wanted to just give it all up. But I kept on hearing in my head, "resist passivity"." Joe said softly.

He took a puff on his cigar and continued, "I was 29-0, and fought George Forman . . . the grill boy. He beat me and I had my first professional loss. I wanted to quit. But I couldn't let passivity get the best of me."

"Talk to me about the 'Thrilla in Manilla'", Pete asked. He felt like a kid asking for the story to be told over and over again.

"It was hot. Really hot", said Joe. "During the fight, Ali said to me, 'They said you were through, Joe'. I said, 'They lied'. At the beginning of the 15th round, Futch stopped the fight. My left eye closed up and I was cut." Joe paused, "Ali was close to quitting. He said that end of the fight was the 'closest thing to dying that I know of.' I wished Eddie had let me go on. I would have beat him, again."

"I had a few fights after that. Even made a cameo appearance in the movie, 'Rocky'. I couldn't compete at a championship level anymore. But I was able to train up and coming boxers. You see, Pete, when you resist being passive, you find other ways to invest in others."

"A lot of young athletes solely depend on their talent and abilities. Oh yea, they are gifted. But they are missing the passion and drive. Too many have been offered the moon to fight. They think its due them. They have their entourage and friends. They got people telling them how great they are. They live in a fantasy world where there ain't no struggle or pain. These guys think they're owed. When that happens, they start to sit back and wait for everything to come to them. They quit. They sit in the corner, even after the bell has rung. They become entitled and passive. Don't do that, Pete. Get after it. And when you get it, don't let it go."

Pete took a long puff on his cigar, nodded his head, and began to consider Smokin' Joe's words. He thought, "you never give in or give up. You can't be passive. You must have a passion. You must find a purpose."

Pete looked at Joe, who was following the trail of his cigar's smoke, "What made you determined to keep on going, Joe?" Frazier looked at Pete, slightly smiled and said, "Life doesn't run away from nobody. Life runs to people. If you're looking for what life has, you'll find it. I was always on the hunt. Always on the prowl. I was the big cat looking for the next challenge. Look for it and you will find it."

"Too many people talk too much", Joe said, "Preaching don't mean you are a true man. You got to go out and do."

"Let me tell you, this," Joe continued, "I wasn't a big guy. People thought the big guys would eat me up. But it was the other way around. I loved to fight bigger guys. My passion. My will. My determination. They were all bigger than the big guys."

"Pete", Joe said in a direct, but instructive tone of voice, "Find the warrior within you. Find the fighter. Fight your fears. Don't worry about the big buys. Don't be passive. Don't be a pushover. Do what you do. It's your passion. It's your purpose. And do it the best you can with all you got. Run hard. Fight to the final bell. Find your passion. Resist passivity."

Joe took a last puff on his cigar and placed it in the ashtray. He looked at Pete and said, "Thanks, brother. I'm ready to hit the road." Joe placed his hands on the arm of the leather chair and started to rise. Pete motioned for him to stop and said, "Joe, I need one thing from you . . .", and Joe stopped him.

"Oh, yea. The cigar band thing. I heard about that from the others." Pete was astounded. "Give me a pen", Joe said. He removed the band from the Kristoff Vengeance, turned it over and wrote, "Resist Passivity" in dark, bold letters.

Joe handed the pen and the cigar band, stood up and said, "Okay, Let's do this. Pete, it was great meeting you and, thank you for the cigar. Kristoff Vengeance? I like that."

Smokin' Joe turned around and walked to the plate glass door. He placed his right hand on the door grip, turned back to Pete, smiled and saluted with two fingers and walked out.

Pete stood motionless trying to process all that had happened. The former World Heavyweight Campion was fading in the sunlight. Pete placed his hands on his hips, shook his head and thought . . . Smokin' Joe Frazier was in The Sanctuary.

Pete looked at the cigar band, walked over to the coffee table, lifted the lid of the humidor. Inside there were no cigars left. Only six cigar bands, and now seven. Each band with a powerful truth that had the potential to turn lives around. He took a moment to think about the day and closed the lid of the humidor.

A humidor made of Mahogany, dark in color with straight grains from the regions of the Congo in Africa. As old as a legacy, withstanding times of poverty and prosperity. Lined with copper, with a rich patina of truth, purity and change. Ornate symbols on each corner made of precious silver, each shaped as an angelic messenger looking up symbolizing hope. And an emblem on top inscribed with the words, "Iron On Iron, Brother To Brother".

Cleaning Up

Pete was trying to process all that had taken place over the past few hours. Had it really been a few hours? He had smoked five or six cigars, which was a pretty normal day. He forgot to each lunch. Also, part of his daily routine. Candidly, Pete had lost track of time.

He looked around The Sanctuary and started doing some of the end-of-day tasks. Pete checked the restroom located behind the sales area. It was clean, paper towels were full, everything seemed in place, as if no one had used it the entire day.

All the ashtrays were clean, except for the two that were in the seating area of the lounge. Pete's ashtray, as well as the same one used by each of the guests needed to be emptied. But that was it. No other ashtrays had been used. Pete took his cleaning cloths, one for the ashtrays and one for the furniture, and began wiping everything down, in preparation for the next day.

He placed the cleaning rags in his back pockets, took a moment to pull up his trousers, and started toward the walk-in humidor. Each day, Pete would survey the cigars in the walk-in. He organized boxes in order of the manufacturer, with usually the bestselling cigars at eye-level or a little higher. He checked for empty boxes, replacing them from backstock, and looked for "stragglers", those cigar boxes that had only one or two left in the box. The stragglers found their way into Pete's pocket for his tomorrow smokes.

After adjusting some of the boxes in the walk-in, and filling some empty spots on the shelves, Pete was done. Everything looked as it should. After exiting the walk-in humidor, Pete grabbed the cleaning rags from his back pocket and tossed them toward the sales area, hitting the sink dead-on.

He walked over to his chair, took a cigar from his pocket and placed it in his mouth, waiting a bit to light it. As he slid into the chair, he sighed a breath of satisfaction.

Pete looked around and The Sanctuary looked good. Nothing had really changed, but it looked different. It felt different. Maybe Pete was seeing it through a different set of eyes, since his guests had shared some amazing truths and thoughts. Maybe Pete had a renewed sense of hope. Pete wasn't certain as to why. But he was confident that things would turnaround.

Pete looked at the plate glass entrance door of The Sanctuary. What had been bright and sunny all day, had now turned to a dark, shadowy ebony of night. Night came quickly, Pete thought.

Pete's head was starting to throb. He hadn't felt any pain all day. Now it was catching up with him. He considered lighting up the cigar that was resting in his mouth but thought he would wait for a few minutes.

As Pete sat in the soft and luxurious leather chair, he eyed the humidor left by Michael. Pete grabbed both arms of the chair and pulled himself forward, toward the coffee table. He placed his hands on each side of the humidor, once again admiring the craftsmanship and quality of such an incredible valued heirloom.

Using both hands, he carefully and slowly lifted the lid. Inside were the seven cigar bands left by his seven guests. Each cigar band had a two- or three-word truth written on the back. Truths that, as Michael had said, could turn around any situation.

Pete looked at the one on top, placed in the humidor last by The Champ. It read, "Resist Passivity". Pete looked at and studied it. These words were rooting their way into Pete's heart. How many times had he decided to "go with the flow" or thought, since everyone else does it that way, he should, too.

Pete thought about what Smokin' Joe had said, "Find the warrior within you. Find the fighter. Fight your fears. Don't worry about the big buys. Don't be passive. Don't be a pushover. Do what you do. It's your passion. It's your purpose. And do it the best you can with all you got. Run hard. Fight to the final bell. Find your passion. Resist passivity."

Pete looked at the cigar band from the Kristoff Vengeance, rotating it in his hand, looking at the front and back. Seeing "Vengeance" on one side and "Resist Passivity" on the other. Pete looked back inside the humidor and saw the other six bands.

He got up, went back to the sales area, grabbed a piece of paper and pen and sat back down in the chair. His head was continuing to hurt, but he also had an idea.

At the top of the paper, Pete wrote the words, "The Sanctuary Is A Place to Find Truth . . . Truth That Can Turn Things Around". He looked at it and underlined, "Truth That Can Turn Things Around". He then took the Vengeance cigar band, turned it over and saw the words on the back.

Directly underneath what Pete had written on the paper, he wrote the words, "Resist Passivity."

Pete then pulled out the next band. It was the band from the Monte Cristo White Label. The Preacher had written the words, "Embrace Eternity" on the back. The Preacher said, "Plan for your everyday, but push for eternity. One is temporary, while the other is permanent. One will vanish, the other will last. One will bring riches and rewards on this earth, the other will bring riches and reward in the heavenlies. Invest in others. Discern deceit. Live wisely. Show mercy. Give grace. Embrace eternity."

Underneath the words, "Resist Passivity", Pete wrote "Embrace Eternity". And placed the Monte Cristo White Series band next to the Kristoff Vengeance band.

Pete, not knowing how this would end, pulled out the next cigar band. It was from a Fuente Best Seller. The Storyteller wrote the words, "Accept Responsibility". He had said, "Every day we are presented with opportunity and opposition. Faith allows us to see and embrace the opportunity. Fear hinders us when we succumb to and envision the fear. Choose faith and combat fear. One will release you to accomplish all that you were created and gifted to do. The other will atrophy your hopes and dreams. Evaluate the opportunities that are before you. With each opportunity comes a new responsibility. Accept responsibility."

Underneath the two other words, Pete wrote, "Accept Responsibility" and placed the Best Seller Cigar band next to the others.

Pete reached in the humidor and pulled out the Perdomo Habano Bourbon Barrel-Aged Connecticut band, with the words, "Lead Courageously" written on the back. The General told Pete, ""Lead yourself before you can lead others. Identify those areas in your life that need improvement and improve them. Read. Journal. Talk with wiser men than you. Learn lessons that you can live and pass to others. A lesson lived is a lesson learned. Be persistent in your purpose. Find courage to stand against foes, fear and failure. When you find this kind of courage, you will lead courageously."

Pete looked at his list. He wrote the words, "Lead Courageously" under "Accept Responsibility", and place the Perdomo cigar band on top of the others.

Retrieving the next one, Pete grabbed the Hoyo de Monterrey cigar band with the words written by The Coach, "Make A Difference". The coach reminded Pete, "Coming alongside of others is a high calling in life. Some call it coaching. Others call it caring. Both exemplify forgetting self and focusing on other. Some say coaching is about making decisions. True coaching is about making a difference. Dads, teachers, priests, pastors, managers, business owners and yes, even coaches will impact lives. When they do, they change a destiny and make a difference."

Pete wrote the words, "Make A Difference", directly underneath "Lead Courageously", "Accept Responsibility", "Embrace Eternity" and "Resist Passivity." He placed the Hoyo band on top of the others.

There were only two cigar bands left in the humidor. Pete recovered the band, with the words, "Encourage Others", from Gracie's Guy's El Producto Queens. Gracie's Guy reminded Pete, "Forget what has happened in the past. Plant seed for the future. Enjoy the encouragement of your friends and family. And look to the future because that's where you're going to spend the rest of your life. Don't take the journey alone. Take others with you. Speak words of hope, not hurt. Always be kind. Encourage others".

Pete wrote the words, "Encourage Others" on the list, right after "Make A Difference". He laid the Queens cigar band with the rest.

There was one cigar band left in the humidor. Pete took out the cigar band from the Aston Prime Minister, with the words, "Never Give Up". The Prime Minister, Mr. Churchill told Pete, "Success is not final. Failure is not final. It is the courage to continue that counts. Be assured that there is always opportunity in every opposition. Never give in. Never give up."

Pete wrote the words, "Never Give Up" as the last line on his sheet of paper.

As Pete read over these powerful words of truth, his eyes got big. He was seeing something that just couldn't be. These words . . . these truths were powerful by themselves, but together . . . Pete stopped, rubbed his eyes because his headache was getting worse.

He looked at the sheet of paper and off to the left of each line, simply wrote the first letter of the first word:

R – Resist Passivity

E – Embrace Eternity

A – Accept Responsibility

L – Lead Courageously

Pete had to stop. The first four letters of the first four phrases spelled the word, real. R-E-A-L. Real as in authentic, the real deal, genuine, true.

Pete went on.

M – Make A Difference

E – Encourage Others

N – Never Give Up

Pete blinked, put his pen down and rubbed his eyes to get some of unclarity out. These seven insights and truths shared by great men, put together in the opposite order of when they came into The Sanctuary . . . the first letter of each truth spells the words, "REAL MEN".

Pete sat in his chair, looking at the humidor, examining the cigar bands and studying the list of seven truths.

This is how he would rebuild and re-envision The Sanctuary. It would be a place where brothers could sharpen and encourage each other, like iron sharpening iron. It would be a place where brothers help brothers become better men. It would be a place to find authentic genuine, real, truth . . . truth that can and will turn lives around.

The Sanctuary would be a place where people are known to resist passivity, embrace eternity, accept responsibility, lead courageously, make a difference, encourage others and never give up.

Pete's head was really starting to hurt. He looked out the plate glass door and it was as dark as he had ever seen. Everything seemed peaceful and quiet. As Pete looked at the paper, he seemed to see the purpose of his eight guests. The last seven providing life-changing lessons of truth. The first guest, giving hope and meaning through the gift of seven cigars and a humidor.

A humidor made of Mahogany, dark in color with straight grains from the regions of the Congo in Africa. As old as a legacy, withstanding times of poverty and prosperity. Lined with copper, with a rich patina of truth, purity and change. Ornate symbols on each corner made of precious silver, each shaped as an angelic messenger looking up symbolizing hope. And an emblem on top inscribed with the words, "Iron On Iron, Brother To Brother".

Pete felt the knot on the back of his head, and it was painful. He closed his eyes to get some needed relief. As Pete sat in his comfortable and luxurious leather chair, he drifted asleep with a sense of hope, peace and contentment.

A Last Visitor

Pete was nearing the end of another day in The Sanctuary. He just finished emptying ashtrays and wiping down tables, after a rush in the lounge. Today was a busy day with sales being good. Customers kept Pete on his toes, today. It had been like this for the past year. Things started turning around the day that Pete moved Michael's humidor to a table, just to the left of the plate glass entrance door. The humidor sat on a small pedestal. Above the humidor, Pete made a poster, framed in dark mahogany wood, to compliment the humidor. The frame has silver corners with a glass front. Inside the frame was a poster that Pete had made. The poster read,

"The Sanctuary Is A Place to Find Truth . . . Truth That Can Turn Things Around", centered at the top.

Below this, read the following:

"R – Resist Passivity"

"E – Embrace Eternity"

"A – Accept Responsibility"

"L – Lead Courageously"

"M – Make A Difference"

"E – Encourage Others"

"N – Never Give Up"

There were no other words or explanation. Just these seven truth-filled statements.

It was not uncommon for people to stop at the plate glass door, take a moment and read the "truths", look back at Pete and give a thumbs-up in agreement.

A number of customers would touch the humidor on the way out as a symbol of respect and identification with the truths. And, still inside the humidor are the seven cigar bands from The Champ, The Preacher, The Storyteller, The General, The Coach, Gracie's Guy and The Prime Minister.

It had been two years since Pete welcomed those seven guests, eight if you include Michael and his humidor. It seemed like yesterday. Pete still recalled waking up the next morning, sitting in his soft, leather chair. His head aching, but not as much as the day before. The knot on the back of his head had gone down. He was fatigued and somewhat confused. Yet, when he looked at the humidor sitting on the coffee table, and saw the seven cigar bands inside, as well as the list of truths he had written, he felt as though everything was going to be okay.

Over the past 24 months, Pete began using the truths written on the back of the cigar bands to reshape The Sanctuary. It was becoming a profitable business and refuge for those who appreciate cigars. There was a Men's Study that met on Tuesday nights and taught guys how to be better men, husbands, fathers and community leaders. There were older men mentoring younger men. Business owners networking with other business owners, not just to generate new business, but to build better businesses. On a regular basis, some customers would collect can goods, clothing and gifts for the underprivileged in the city.

This was a part of resisting passivity, embracing eternity and making a difference.

Pete continued to share information with his employees, asking them how The Sanctuary could better meet the needs of its guests. He asked customers what they liked about The Sanctuary and what he could do to improve it and make it better.

This was a part of leading courageously and accepting responsibility.

Pete invited positive conversation, even if there were differing points of view, everyone had a right to share their thoughts and beliefs, as long as there was deference to others and respect for all. Handshakes and fist-bumps were common to see after there had been a long discussion. And even an occasional hug between brothers.

This was a part of encouraging others.

And Pete was committed to making it work. It didn't matter if things got tough or challenging, Pete decided he was going to make it work and stick it out.

This was a part of never giving up.

These kind of positive actions and decisive decisions had not only changed the way The Sanctuary operated as a business, but it also has had an impacted on the way guest felt welcomed, cared for and appreciated.

Pete walked toward the plate glass door, looked at the humidor sitting on the pedestal, placed his own hand on it and re-read, for probably the thousandth time, the truths listed with the framed poster.

"R – Resist Passivity"

"E – Embrace Eternity"

"A – Accept Responsibility"

"L – Lead Courageously"

"M – Make A Difference"

"E – Encourage Others"

"N – Never Give Up"

Pete was creating a business and culture where real men could find themselves, be confident and comfortable, and continue to be the best men they could be.

Pete smiled in humble appreciation, tapped the top of the humidor and went to sit in his chair, smoke a cigar and enjoy the rest of the remaining day.

As he almost made it to his chair, Pete heard the creak of the hinge of the plate glass door at the entrance of The Sanctuary. As he turned, he saw a younger man with a soulful stride. He seemed confident and composed.

Pete made his way to the door. As the younger man came closer, Pete noticed that he was a light colored, black man. Late twenties to early thirties, with short cropped and trimmed hair. He wore a long sleeve lined shirt with the sleeves rolled up to just above his elbows. He had on light colored jeans, neat and stylish. He had a leather bracelet, as well as a beaded bracelet on this right wrist, and a chronograph on his left wrist. As Pete looked at the man, he noticed his shoes. He wasn't wearing socks and his shoes were a blue and white saddle shoes with interlacing blue and white shoestrings.

Pete looked at the young man and said, "Hey, my friend. Welcome to The Sanctuary. I'm here to make your day great."

The young man offered his hand to shake and said, "Thank you, sir. My name is Matthew." "I'm glad you're here." said Pete, "Several guests just left, it's just me, for the moment. So that gives us plenty of time to sit, talk and enjoy a cigar."

Matthew nodded in agreement and took a quite visual survey of the shop. As they were standing, Pete couldn't take his eyes off Matthew's shoes. "Matthew, may I ask you a question that may seem a bit odd?" "Of course," he replied.

Pete continued, "I'm admiring your shoes. I've only seen one other pair like them. They were the same color and had the same shoestrings." Pete really didn't ask a formal question. He just left the comment about the shoes hanging out there. Matthew smiled, "Thank you, Pete. These shoes are somewhat of a family tradition." Matthew didn't elaborate and Pete wondered.

Pete offered Matthew a chair in the lounge area, next to his. Pete invited him, "Would you like to join me and have a cigar?" motioning to the chairs, Pete's and the one that had been used by the guests almost two years ago.

Matthew said, "I'd really like that, Pete. But could I ask you a question?" "Yes," said Pete, "Anything." Matthew turned his attention to the left side of the front door.

Calmly and with great inquiry, Matthew said, "The humidor? I've only seen one other like it, in a photograph. It looks as though it has great meaning and tradition. Please tell me about it."

Pete paused. He didn't know where to start or what to say. From the beginning, he told Matthew of the night when a gentleman came in The Sanctuary, told Pete his story and gifted him the humidor. He continued telling Matthew about the seven cigars inside the humidor and the instructions for Pete to give them away, telling the recipients that an old man wanted to bless them.

Matthew nodded as if to signal for Pete to continue. The words just came flowing out of Pete.

He went on to talk about the seven guest who came in. Each cigar, in the exact order they were placed in the humidor, was perfectly chosen for each person. And he told Matthew about the seven truths each man wrote on the back of his cigar band. Pete then shared that when he pulled the cigars bands out of the humidor, in the exact order they were put in, that the first letter of each truth spelled "REAL MEN".

Matthew was nodding and smiling. Pete told him that these truths have not only changed his own life, the life of The Sanctuary, but has also impacted hundreds of customers.

Matthew waited for Pete's energy to subside and said, "What an amazing story. I'd like you to tell me more. But, how about that cigar?"

Pete was a bit embarrassed that he went on and on about the humidor. He quickly motioned for Matthew to sit and, with a sense of apology said, "Matthew, today's cigar is on me. What can I get you?" Matthew said, "Pick one out for me. Find something that may be new to me." Pete knew exactly what to get.

Pete excused himself, walked into the humidor, went to the second shelf from the top on the left-hand side and selected a Rocky Patel Disciple. Pete grabbed two.

Sitting down in his chair, Pete handed the Disciple cigar to Matthew and said, "This is an excellent cigar. It features tobacco from Nicaragua, and it has a Mexican San Andres wrapper. It's medium to full-bodied, and it is full of subtle flavors. It's one of my favorites."

Pete motioned for Matthew to use the table cutter and lighter. They both lit their cigars and took a first puff.

Matthew, enjoying the Disciple cigar, looked over and said, "Pete, tell me about the gentlemen who gifted you with such an interesting humidor. The story is amazing." Pete nodded in agreement and said, "His name was Michael. His great-grandfather was a slave for a family named the Shepherds. The Shepherds ended up giving Michaels family freedom and land to build their own dream. It really is an unbelievable story."

Pete paused and remembered the importance of encouraging others. He also wanted to make a positive difference in Matthew's life. Pete took another puff on his cigar and said, "Matthew, tell me about yourself. What brings you The Sanctuary?"

Matthew took a puff on his cigar, placed it in the ashtray nearest his chair, slid forward said, "Pete, I am from a family of slaves from the Congo region of Africa. My great-great grandfather was given the name 'Solomon' by the owner of the plantation where he worked. My great grandfather was a wood worker of fine Mahogany. His name was Noah. And my grandfather gave me these shoes. His name was Michael."

Matthew paused, to not only catch his breath, but to take another puff on his cigar. "My great-grandfather made that humidor by hand", pointing to the pedestal on the left-hand side of the glass door. "He used wood that came over from Africa harvested from the same ship that transported my great-great-grandfather. The copper is from a teapot used by my great-great-grandmother. The silversmith work is by my great-grandfather. And the emblem was crafted by my grandfather." Pete couldn't say a word. He just looked at Matthew.

"You asked me what brings me here, today?", said Matthew. "I think I know the reason, Pete. When Grandfather gifted you the humidor, he didn't have anyone in his family to leave it to. My parents had a difficulty becoming pregnant. Always wanting a family, my Mom and Dad decided to adopt. I was the chosen child. I believe I'm here to tell you that the path you have chosen and the truths you have claimed are good and right. These truths will turn lives around. They have done it in my family for many generations."

Pete was silent. He had so many things to say but couldn't find any words. He just looked at Matthew.

"Pete", Matthew continued, "My grandfather's name means 'Gift from God'. I know that he was a gift to you from the Almighty. My name, 'Matthew', means 'Gift of God'. I am a result of the hard work, belief and commitment instilled in me by my grandfather. And love, compassion and acceptance shown to me by my adoptive parents."

Pete was overwhelmed with emotion.

Matthew extended both of his arms and turned them over to reveal tattoos on both wrists. Using his right hand, he pointed to the underside of his left wrist. There in all capital letters was the word, REAL. Matthew said, "R-E-A-L. Resist passivity. Embrace eternity. Accept responsibility. Lead courageously. These are truths that were taught to me by my grandfather and now I am teaching my son." Using his left hand, he pointed to the underside of his right wrist. The in all capital letters was the word, MEN. Matthew said, "M-E-N. Make a difference. Encourage others. Never give up. You are making a difference in the lives of men, just like my grandfather made a difference in your life. As you continue to encourage others; never quit, never give up."

Pete looked at both wrists. He was without words. Humbled. Overcome. Honored.

Matthew slid back in his chair, retrieved his cigar and took a puff. He blew out the smoke, looked at the band of the cigar and turned to Pete.

"Pete", he said, "you have selected the perfect cigar for us to share. It's Rocky Patel's Disciple. A disciple is a follower who also leads others to truth. They guide others out of darkness into light. They walk the path of those who have led the way and invite others to join them on the journey."

"Disciples", said Pete. "Disciples", replied Matthew. Pete nodded.

Both men sat there for just a minute or two, reflecting on all that had just taken place.

Pete took a puff on his cigar, Matthew and said, "Hey. I want you to take the humidor back. It's part of your family's heritage and legacy."

Matthew smiled, shaking his head, "No, Pete. Grandfather left it for you. He knew that you would have a greater opportunity to share the gift of these seven truths more than he would have. Imagine how many men will walk by those truths each and every day, and be challenged to be real men; authentic, true and genuine men."

Matthew took a draw on his cigar and removed the band that read "Disciple" and placed it in the change pocket of his jeans. He took one last puff and placed the cigar on the ashtray's stirrup.

He stood and said, "Pete, come with me to the humidor. There's something I need to show you."

Pete quickly stood, place his cigar on the ashtray next to his chair and followed Matthew to the front of the store, to the left of the plate glass door and to the pedestal on which the humidor sat. Matthew opened the lid of the humidor and gently removed an inside tray that Pete never knew existed. Underneath the tray was a round coin-like medallion a little bit larger that a turn-of-the-century silver dollar.

Pete was astounded. He asked Matthew, "What is it?" "It's called a challenge coin," Matthew said. Pete just shook his head as if this was something brand new to him.

Matthew continued, "A challenge coin is a small medallion, bearing an organization's insignia or emblem and highlight its mission. These coins are carried by the organization's most loyal and faithful members."

Matthew explained, "Traditionally, they are given to authenticate membership, honor commitment, and recognize loyalty or achievements. A challenge coin identifies, it instructs, and it inspires. Receiving a coin is a rare and worthy honor."

The coin was a bright bronze, almost gold color. It was accented with navy blue on each side. On one side in the center with raised letters in blue read, "Iron on Iron", and underneath it the reference, "Prov 27:17". Around the edged blue rim were the words, "Resist Passivity", "Embrace Eternity", "Accept Responsibility" and "Lead Courageously". On the other side, in the center were the raised letters, in blue that read, "Brother to Brother". Around the edge of the coin was a rim with the words, "Make A Difference", "Encourage Others" and "Never Give Up".

The coin was weighty and significant.

Matthew handed the coin to Pete and said, "Now you can carry these truths with you wherever you go. They will remind you what is required of real men."

Pete looked at Matthew. He was so grateful. He told Matthew, "I can't take this from you. You've already told me to keep the humidor." Matthew pointed to the underside of his wrists showing his tattoos, smiled and then reached into his change pocket of his jeans. Matthew pulled out a matching challenge coin. He said, "My grandfather gave this to me when I turned eighteen. He wanted me to always remember what it takes for men to be real men."

Matthew held his challenge coin in his right hand showing it to Pete. Pete held his challenge coin in his right-hand showing Matthew. Both men, without any prompting, shook hands. The clanging of the coins was music to both their ears.

Each placed their coins back in their pockets, as a daily reminder to be real men.

Pete placed his arms on Matthew's shoulders. They gave each other a big bear hug and each whispered in the other's ear, "Real Men".

Matthew turned, placed his left hand on the humidor and and his right hand on over his heart. He looked up heavenly and pointed, giving him a thumbs up. He walked out the door, wearing his blue and white saddle shoes with matching shoelaces.

Pete watched Matthew through the plate glass door. His heart was full.

He reached in his pocket with his right hand and felt the round, weighty challenge coin that read, "Brother to Brother, Iron on Iron".

He placed his left hand on the humidor that started it all, and looked up toward the heavenlies with a grateful heart. A humidor made of Mahogany, dark in color with straight grains from the regions of the Congo in Africa. As old as a legacy, withstanding times of poverty and prosperity. Lined with copper, with a rich patina of truth, purity and change. Ornate symbols on each corner made of precious silver, each shaped as an angelic messenger looking up symbolizing hope. And an emblem on top inscribed with the words, "Iron On Iron, Brother To Brother".

Turn Around Truths

Resist Passivity – "Smokin" Joe Frazier

"Find the warrior within you. Find the fighter. Fight your fears. Don't worry about the big buys. Don't be passive. Don't be a pushover. Do what you do. It's your passion. It's your purpose. And do it the best you can with all you got. Run hard. Fight to the final bell. Find your passion. Resist passivity."

Embrace Eternity – Charles S. Spurgeon

"Plan for your everyday, but push for eternity. One is temporary, while the other is permanent. One will vanish, the other will last. One will bring riches and rewards on this earth, the other will bring riches and reward in the heavenlies. Invest in others. Discern deceit. Live wisely. Show mercy. Give grace. Embrace eternity."

Accept Responsibility – Samuel Clemens (Mark Twain)

"Every day we are presented with opportunity and opposition. Faith allows us to see and embrace the opportunity. Fear hinders us when we succumb to and envision the fear. Choose faith and combat fear. One will release you to accomplish all that you were created and gifted to do. The other will atrophy you hopes and dreams. Evaluate the opportunities that are before you. With each opportunity comes a new responsibility. Accept responsibility."

Lead Courageously – Ulysses S. Grant"

"Lead yourself before you can lead others. Identify those areas in your life that need improvement and improve them. Read. Journal. Talk with wiser men than you. Learn lessons that you can live and pass to others. A lesson lived is a lesson learned. Be persistent in your purpose. Find courage to stand against foes, fear and failure. When you find this kind of courage, you will lead courageously."

Make A Difference - Red Auerbach

"Coming alongside of others is a high calling in life. Some call it coaching. Others call it caring. Both exemplify forgetting self and focusing on other. Some say coaching is about making decisions. True coaching is about making a difference. Dads, teachers, priests, pastors, managers, business owners and yes, even coaches will impact lives. When they do, they change a destiny and make a difference."

Encourage Others - George Burns

"Forget what has happened in the past. Plant seeds for the future. Enjoy the encouragement of your friends and family. And look to the future because that's where you're going to spend the rest of your life. Don't take the journey alone. Take others with you. Speak words of hope, not hurt. Always be kind. Encourage others."

Never Give Up - Winston Churchill

"Success is not final. Failure is not final. It is the courage to continue that counts. Be assured that there is always opportunity in every opposition. Never give in. Never give up."

"The Sanctuary Is A Place to Find Truth . . . Truth That Can Turn Things Around"

R - Reject Passivity
E – Embrace Eternity
A – Accept Responsibility
L – Lead Courageously

M – Make A Difference
E – Encourage Others
N – Never Give Up

The Back Story

Jessamyn West writes, "Fiction reveals truth that reality obscures." The fictional account of Pete and The Sanctuary, as told as *"Iron & Leaf"* reveals truth from similarities of different cigar businesses.

This story is an amalgamation of two cigar shops, both located in Central Virginia. City Place Cigar, established in 2009, and Pap's Cigar Company, established in 2018. Both shops, at different times, have occupied the same space on 817 Main Street. City Place Cigar ceased to exist after several years in business. Pap's Cigar Company is currently thriving as it serves cigar aficionados from the community and truly treats them as guests.

The character of Pete is a blending of both proprietors of these establishments. Rick Smith and me. Rick currently runs the day-to-day operations of Pap's. He is the face, heartbeat and soul of Pap's. In my 65 plus years, I have seen and experienced more local shops that I can count. By comparison, Rick is one of the most experienced entrepreneurs and savvy small business owners I have ever met.

If you visit Lynchburg, Virginia, nestled just below the Blue Ridge Mountains, you will appreciate the Old Dominion's finest. Walk into Pap's Cigar Co. located at 817 Main Street, and you will hear the plate glass door click as it opens. As you enter, you will see the walk-in humidor on your left, including the high shelves holding back stock, and a step ladder that Rick uses to reach the top shelf . . . everyone watching to make sure he doesn't fall. To the right of the walk-in humidor's door is the Cigar Indian. Rick sits in the same chair every day. And, if I am visiting, I'm in the chair directly across from him.

You will hear Rick greet every guest, welcoming them and tell them to take their time . . . "The humidor is open until 10 o'clock. Stay as long as you like. I'll come and get you before we leave." Rick is the consummate conversationalist. He asks the best questions to encourage all to respond and engage. I've often said that when you sit down and light a cigar, you have almost an hour to talk and meet a friend.

And, Rick has "stragglers" in his pocket.

Although the shop is called Pap's Cigar Company, the private membership lounge in the back is called, "The Sanctuary".

If you visit, you will notice the sales area, maybe see the rag that Rick uses to clean ashtrays, and behind the sales counter, you can see a picture of Bob Ott, or "Pap" in Yankee Pinstripes, ballcap and smoking a cigar.

In the early years of City Place Cigar, we focused on building a community where men could find refuge and encouragement.

One of our early customers and employees, Jimmy Lewis wrote an article for the prestigious *"Institute For Faith, Work & Economics"* in August, 2018 entitled, "Cigar Smoking and the Glory of God". Jimmy wrote, *"The simultaneously intimidating and liberating nature of an environment like this is that conversations are frequently deep, and people are not shy about challenging your ideas or views. As a result, there is trust, candor, and confidentiality."*

He continued, *"Because of this 'fraternity'—by this I mean in the classical sense, brotherhood - employees and customers were not merely employees and customers, they were (and still are) close friends. Spending a few hours together every day for years made us more than lawyers, college students, veterans, businessmen, and bankers; it made us equals, mentors/mentees, and friends. Once you walk into the shop, you're immediately able to vent, ask for advice, or simply enjoy the company of people that respect you and one another. This is the environment we used as staff members to love and lead people toward Jesus, and we were told regularly by people who found churches too judgmental or intimidating that we provided a community they had never experienced."*

One of the highlights in the early days of our shop was a weekly study. During these times, with thirty to forty men, we discussed how our lives could be modeled after Jesus' thirty-three years on this earth. We learned His example of honoring His Heavenly Father in our relationships and vocations.

For younger guys, it was an opportunity to hear from men one to two generations older, hear about their struggles through life, and what they learned along the way through leading families and running businesses. For older guys, it was an opportunity to hear from men their sons' and grandsons' ages about their struggles with family, school, figuring out the future, and what God's will for their lives may be.

These relationships gave all of us opportunities to glean wisdom from men in all walks of life and to be transparent and trusting with men who started as acquaintances but who became brothers.

I have a tattoo on the underside of my left wrist that reads, "REAL". And, I still carry around a challenge coin from City Place Cigar with the meaning of REAL on one side.

Foundational pillars of being REAL MEN are found in the first four letters. Too many times, we know what we need to do, but to do it requires sacrifice, self-denial and hard work. **Resisting passivity**, or in many cases, rejecting passivity is the first step to being who we were designed to be. **Embracing eternity** allows me to see who I am and where I am heading. Over the years, I am amazed at the complexity and intricate design of our bodies, soul and mind. Look around at look at massive buildings . . . there is always an architect or designer. Every work of art has an artist. Every book has an author. Every recipe has a chef. I cannot ignore the reality that each of us is unique, complex, intricate and functioning. I am who I am because of a Master Designer. We are designed or created to experience our Creator. Often because of self-centered choices or resting in passivity, we get "off course". Our choices lead us away from God's design to areas of brokenness. We try to escape or numb the pain of brokenness in many ways. Brokenness causes us to realize that something has to change, yet the changes we try to make are superficial and short-lived.

Since this kind of change doesn't come from inside us, it has to come from somewhere else. Through love, grace and mercy, our Creator gives us the opportunity to turn our lives around. Through a recognition of God, we can again find our purpose and meaning and finally fix the brokenness. This is good news and it is found in the most well-known passage of Scripture, penned over 2,000 years ago, "For this is how God loved the world: He gave his one and only Son, so that everyone who believes in him will not perish but have eternal life." (John 3:16 NLT)

We can discover who we are by experiencing who Jesus is.

Once a man resists passivity and embraces eternity, he is ready to **accept responsibility** in his role of manhood and leadership and in turn, **lead courageously**. He stands to protect his family, make tough decisions and set the pace for all to follow.

To find our more, check out my friend Tierce Green at **tiercegreen.com** Or, feel free to email me at bob@servantone.com

The 7 turnaround truths that spell out the acrostic, REAL MEN have been tested and tried. They work.

It's my hope that this fictional work, *"Iron & Leaf"*, has revealed some truth that is clear, true and no longer obscure.

So, if you get a chance to stop by 817 Main Street, in downtown Lynchburg, Virginia, stop by and say "hi" to Rick. You'll be glad you did.

Acknowledgments

Debbie, thank you for allowing me to pursue this hobby and interest. You are my favorite to take to a new shop.

Travis, thank you for your support, brother. I remember the day we each sat in different parking lots and talked about the future. The future is here and we're sprinting to eternity. Let's go reach the men of Northern Kentucky.

Jacob, my new friend and brother. Monday night Thrive. Thank you for your encouragement. Thanks for being a loving father to those who needed a dad.

Reagan, you are an inspiration and a pacesetter for those who have a dream to create an incredible environment for cigars. Your innovation, insight and passion for this industry are like none other. To say. "I am proud of you" doesn't even come close to the admiration and respect you hold in my heart. You and Randy have created a cigar refuge in "The Cigar Mansion". Tuscaloosa is lucky to have "R & R".

Darian "Jack" Jackson, thank you for your leadership in *Brothers Of The Leaf (Online Community)* on Facebook. Way to grow this group. You are one amazing young man. Thanks for being one of the REAL MEN. Go Dapper D's.

To my grandsons, this is why Poppy enjoys cigars.

To the team that was a part of City Place Cigar, thank you for buying into the Kingdom vision. Yes. I said Vision.

Rick Smith, thank you for continuing the legacy in Lynchburg. Some of my best conversations have been with you. Thank you for letting me create the story of *"Iron & Leaf"* with you. You are an incredible encouragement and advisor. I hope to spend eternity with you, Brother. "As iron sharpens iron, so one man sharpens another." (Proverbs 27:17) You are a dear friend who sharpens me . . . and an incredible aficionado.

Made in the USA
Columbia, SC
12 October 2023

24355338R00074